# Jimmy Stillman, I will always love you

A NOVEL

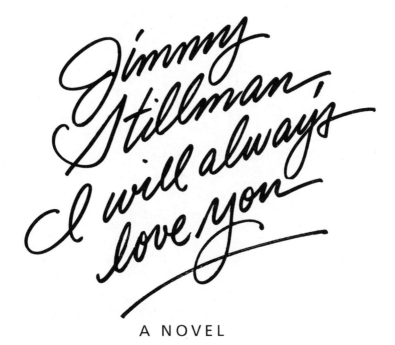

A NOVEL

**ERIC HENDERSHOT**

**BOOKCRAFT**
Salt Lake City, Utah

*To*
*Dickilyn*

*I will always love you.*

Library of Congress Catalog Card Number: 94-78193
ISBN 0-88494-949-4

First Printing, 1994

Printed in the United States of America

## Special Thanks

To my family, especially to my wife, Dickilyn, and my daughter Hayley, for their special insight and talents.

To my father for all the stories over the years.

To Richard and Verna Johnson for their untiring support and encouragement.

To my brother Chris—the real "King of the River."

To Elaine Cannon for encouraging me to submit this story to Bookcraft.

# 1

The sun was just beginning to peek over the top of Table Rock Mountain when the Mooneys' loaded station wagon pulled to a stop in front of Jimmy Stillman's house.

"Don't be long, sweetheart," said Ted Mooney to his eleven-year-old daughter, Linda, who was sitting in the backseat next to her older brother, Paul.

Linda was too sad to answer. Her heart was heavy today, heavier than it had ever been. Her father had accepted a promotion with his company in Glendale, California, and this meant she was leaving Towanda, Pennsylvania, for good. The other family members were excited about the move, but she couldn't be.

Linda slid out the back door, closed it behind her, and walked slowly toward the side of the house. *It should be Jimmy coming to my house to say good-bye,* she thought to herself as she reached the spot directly under Jimmy's second-story bedroom window. But it didn't really matter, because chances were that she would never see Jimmy Stillman again. California might as well be on the other side of the world when you're only eleven.

Linda knew it was too early for Jimmy to be up, so she gathered some pebbles from beneath a large lilac bush and, with careful aim, began tossing them at his window. Soon the curtains parted, and Jimmy Stillman looked down at Linda.

Linda was just about to throw another pebble when she saw him. Her heart skipped a beat, then began to flutter. Jimmy opened the window and poked his head out.

No wonder her heart beat so—he was a handsome boy, with a full head of dark brown hair and soft brown eyes the color of the horse chestnuts that grew on the big tree in front of Linda's house. She had described Jimmy's eyes to her mother: "And when he smiles, Mom, they twinkle. They really do."

But this morning there wasn't much twinkle in Jimmy Stillman's eyes. He was still half asleep.

"Whaddya want?" he asked, a little irritated.

"I'm moving to California, remember?"

"Oh yeah," said Jimmy, remembering. He cleared his throat, trying to get rid of a small frog.

"We're all packed and on our way. I just came to say good-bye."

There was a long, uncomfortable pause as Jimmy rubbed his eyes and Linda tried to think of what to say next.

"How far did you say you're gonna live from the ocean?" Jimmy finally asked.

"My dad says it's only an hour away."

"Cool."

There was really nothing else to say except good-bye, but Linda couldn't bring herself to say it. She took a deep breath. "Well, I guess I better be going."

"Have fun in California," said Jimmy.

"Say good-bye to everybody for me. Okay?"

"Okay."

Linda's mother, Carolyn, rolled down her window and called out, "C'mon, honey, we've gotta go."

Linda turned and motioned to her mother that she would be just a moment longer. She looked back up at Jimmy. "Good-bye, Jimmy."

" 'Bye. It was nice knowin' ya."

"It was nice knowing you too. Good luck with your fishin'."

The last thing Linda wanted to do was cry. She turned her head and started to walk away just in time before Jimmy could see the huge tears that welled up in her eyes, then overflowed and cascaded down her cheeks. She felt an emptiness inside that she had never experienced before. A plain good-bye just wasn't good enough—at least, not good enough for Jimmy Stillman. There were too many special memories to have it all end with just a simple, dumb good-bye. What did it really matter if Jimmy saw her crying?

She whirled around and blurted out what she really came to say. "I love you, Jimmy Stillman. I always will! I'm gonna miss you more than all my friends put together."

She looked up at Jimmy one last time, tears still coursing down her red face, then she turned and ran to the car as fast as she could.

Jimmy leaned out of the window. "I'm gonna miss you too," he called out after her.

But Linda didn't hear. If she only had, it would have made her trip to California a lot easier.

# 2

Linda didn't look up again until she heard the hum and drone of the tires as the station wagon crossed the Towanda bridge. She couldn't leave Towanda without seeing the river one last time.

Beneath the bridge flowed the beautiful blue-green waters of the Susquehanna. For more than four hundred miles this river made its way from central New York State through Pennsylvania and Maryland to the Chesapeake Bay. Linda wished there were some magical way she could take the Susquehanna to California with her. *But then, what fun would the river be without Jimmy?* she thought. Everything about the river reminded her of him.

On hot summer days she and Jimmy would roll up their pant legs and hunt for crayfish under the rocks along the shore. When they had gathered enough they would use them for bait to catch bass, perch, or bluegills under the James Street bridge in north Towanda. Linda couldn't count the times she was awakened early on a Saturday morning before sunrise by pebbles hitting the side of the house. She would crawl out of bed half asleep and stumble barefoot to the window. Below, standing next to the birdbath, would be Jimmy, with a fishing pole in one hand and an old, dented tackle box in the other, wanting to know if she wanted to go fishing. Whether she went with him or not, Jimmy always seemed to come home after dark with his limit. It was a known fact that he knew the river better than any other fisherman in Bradford County, and he was only eleven years old. Seasoned fishermen were always knocking on his door, asking where the best spots were to catch walleyed pike or rock bass. And Jimmy always had an answer for them. Linda's dad kiddingly called him "the river rat."

Jimmy's reputation for knowing the river was enhanced during the spring of '86. A terrible accident took place the winter of that year just twenty miles upriver from Towanda, near the town of Athens, Pennsylvania. In a driving snowstorm, an automobile carrying two women slid off the highway, crashed through the guardrail, and plunged into the icy waters of the river. One of the women managed to get out of the car and swim to shore. When the car was dredged up from the bottom of the river, it was empty—the other woman was somewhere in the river. An all-out effort to find her was unsuccessful.

When Linda's mother read about it on the front page of the *Towanda Daily Review,* she made a prediction. "Mark my words," she declared, "if anyone finds that woman it will be Jimmy Stillman."

Several days later Jimmy woke Linda before sunrise to see if she wanted to go fishing.

"I want to, but it's so-o-o early," she said with a tired yawn.

"You don't catch the big ones in bed," Jimmy replied, then he disappeared alone in the direction of the river. The next day, when Linda read about Jimmy finding the woman's body, she was glad she had stayed in bed the previous morning.

Jimmy was the local hero for about a week after that. He was even interviewed by Jack Barnes on WTTC, Towanda's one and only radio station.

After Jimmy got his own boat, Linda spent even more time with him. The boat was a homemade one he had bought at a garage sale for twenty-five dollars. With his dad's help he made some minor repairs and patched the leaks with black roof tar. It floated, and it never took in a drop.

Linda would never forget the day Jimmy invited her to go on the boat's maiden voyage. "Where do you wanna go?" he had asked, trying not to show too much excitement.

Linda gazed out to the lush green island that split the waters of the Susquehanna near the railroad bridge. Ever since she could remember, it had been her dream to explore that island.

Before she could answer, Jimmy said, "The island, right?"

"That's right. How'd ya know?"

"C'mon, get in," was all Jimmy said.

For nearly twenty minutes Jimmy rowed the boat for all he was worth. The closer they got to the island, the faster Linda's heart beat.

As they pulled the boat from the water onto the beach, Linda was the first to speak. "I kinda feel like the Swiss Family Robinson or Christopher Columbus. Don't you?"

Jimmy didn't answer; he just looked at her and smiled. His eyes twinkled, and Linda could feel the blood rush into her cheeks.

"C'mon," said Jimmy, "let's take a look."

Almost immediately they came across some carp that had been trapped in a small pond when the river receded. The pond was stagnating, and if the scavengers weren't removed and put back into the river, their fate would be certain. Linda sat on the bank and watched Jimmy chase the carp down, wrestle with them, then throw them into the river. He saved the biggest for last. It was an old granddaddy that easily weighed forty pounds.

Linda screamed and hollered, jumped up and down, and cheered as Jimmy chased that old monster up and down the pond. Several times Jimmy had the fish in his grasp, but each time the huge, slimy devil would wriggle free and escape.

Finally, exhausted and angry, Jimmy gave up. He shouted at the top of his lungs as the fish swam away for what seemed like the hundredth time, "Go ahead and die, you big, dumb, ugly fish!" He turned and started to stomp out of the water, slipping several times and going completely under. When he reached the bank, he was wet to the bone. He fell back on the grass, out of breath, and closed his eyes.

"Stupid, dumb fish, stupid, dumb fish," he repeated over and over to himself. He was so frustrated Linda was sure he was going to cry. But then, all of a sudden, he sat straight up and glared out at the pond. His dark brown eyes narrowed and went black. His jaw turned to stone. He jumped to his feet, ready to fight.

"No dumb fish, even if it weighs a thousand pounds, is gonna beat Jimmy Stillman, king of the river," he cried. Without taking his eyes off the pond he peeled off his wet shirt that reeked of the monster and his friends and handed it to Linda. He ran his fingers through his wet hair and marched back to the pond. Linda couldn't remember when he had looked so handsome.

Once in the murky water, Jimmy began to slowly and deliberately stalk the monster. Linda sat down on the bank, clutching his wet shirt and trying to contain her excitement. The huge fish seemed to somehow sense Jimmy's determination and was up for the challenge. Like a big, playful dog, it faced Jimmy, tail wagging, ready for the game to begin.

When Jimmy got within striking distance he positioned himself, counted to three, then dived at the monster. Linda sprang to her feet and looked out at the muddy water. Jimmy surfaced, both fists oozing with thick, black mud. "Where'd he go? Where'd he go?" he shouted, rubbing the mud and water from his eyes.

"There, over there!" Linda screamed, pointing to the far end of the pond. There the old devil was, swimming lazily in about four feet of water near the edge of the pond. Jimmy hurried to the pond's edge and climbed out.

"What are you gonna do?" Linda asked.

Without taking his eyes off the fish, Jimmy motioned for Linda to be still. Then, without a word, he took off in a dead run. A few feet from the water, he went airborne. There was a tremendous splash as he hit the water's surface. Bull's-eye! The fish never knew what hit him. Down they both went, hitting the bottom of the pond with Jimmy on top. It was a perfectly executed double fin takedown. Jimmy had the huge scavenger pinned. The powerful monster struggled to free himself, but Jimmy "King of the River" Stillman would not be denied this time. With every bit of strength he could muster, he held on.

On the bank Linda stood frozen with excitement, staring down at the swirling, muddy eddy created by the violent battle beneath. The few seconds Jimmy had been under the water seemed like minutes to her. She kept whispering to herself, "C'mon, Jimmy, c'mon."

And then, suddenly Jimmy emerged, gasping for air. In his skinny arms was the biggest, wildest fish Linda had ever seen.

"Hold on tight, Jimmy," she shouted.

Jimmy squeezed the monster harder, then shot a triumphant look at Linda as he headed for dry ground. In a wet trail of glory, he hurried to the river as fast as he could, trying with all his might not to drop the squirming fish. Linda chased after them.

In a quiet little cove banked with dark gray mud,

Jimmy eased into the water until he was waist deep, then slowly submerged the big fish. "Go on, get outta here, you big, dumb fish." He gave the monster a gentle shove. The fish nonchalantly, and without the least bit of gratitude, swam away.

Jimmy and Linda seemed to be mesmerized by the gentle movements of the big fish as it slowly made its way to deeper waters. The moment was so peaceful and quiet. The only thing that could be heard was the sound of water dripping from Jimmy's wet hands into the river.

When the fish finally disappeared from view, Jimmy turned and looked back toward the bank at Linda. Their eyes met and held. Neither spoke for a long moment—it was almost as if anything they might say would spoil it.

At last, Jimmy spoke, his voice calm and peaceful. "I think from now on we should call this place Freedom Cove. What do you think?"

Linda thought about it. "I like that," she finally answered.

Suddenly the threatening sound of thunder in the not-too-far distance broke the silence. Jimmy and Linda looked up. Somehow during all the excitement they had both failed to notice the large storm clouds that had blackened the summer sky. A gust of wind raced up the river, frightening a kingfisher from its perch in a nearby tree and nearly chilling Jimmy to the bone. A bolt of lightning ripped a jagged seam across the dark sky. Almost simultaneously a tremendous clap of thunder exploded overhead. Linda screamed with fright, and Jimmy hurried from the river. Together they ran with all their might across the island to the bank where they had beached Jimmy's small boat. As they were about to set sail, the black clouds burst open and a heavy, driving rain began to fall.

"We can't go across in this," Linda shouted over the wind and rain.

Jimmy looked about for a moment, thinking.

"C'mon, give me a hand," he shouted. Together they took hold of the boat and dragged it even farther up the bank to where a large tree had fallen. With one quick motion they turned the little boat over and leaned it against the tree, and in an instant they were under the boat, protected from the storm.

The pounding, pelting rain against the bottom of the boat sounded like the rat-tat-tat of machine-gun fire. Linda brushed her wet hair away from her eyes and looked over at Jimmy, who was hugging himself, trying to keep warm. A huge smile washed across her wet face.

Jimmy looked at her. "What's so funny?"

"Nothing."

"Then why are you smiling?"

"I don't know. I guess I'm just happy. I think this is the best day I've ever had."

A smile started at the corners of Jimmy's mouth and spread across his face. His dark eyes twinkled and lit Linda's soul.

# 3

The pounding of the rain on top of the station wagon and the steady beat of the windshield wipers brought Linda back to the harsh reality that she was leaving her life in Towanda behind. She looked over at her fourteen-year-old brother, Paul, who was fast asleep, mouth gaping open. He disgusted her. Paul was actually excited about moving to California. For him, California meant the Dodgers, Angels, Lakers, Disneyland, and the beach. How could he possibly want to leave Towanda for the crush and rush of stupid Los Angeles? Linda had always thought Paul was kind of dumb. Now she was sure of it.

She leaned her head back against the seat and closed her eyes, remembering the very first time she ever saw Jimmy. It was in the fourth grade at Mulberry Street Elementary School. Jimmy and his father came to the classroom to meet Mrs. Carroll, the fourth grade teacher. Jimmy stood tall and straight in front of the class, pretending not to be nervous, but Linda could tell he was. She had always been able to read him, right from the start.

After his father left, Mrs. Carroll introduced Jimmy to the class, then told him to take the vacant seat in the third row. Linda was excited—the vacant seat was right across from her. That first day Linda spent more time watching Jimmy than she did Mrs. Carroll.

When school was out that afternoon Linda followed Jimmy home to find out where he lived. She discovered that he lived in a small gray house on Poplar Street, just two blocks from the school. Just as he was about to step up onto his porch he turned and caught Linda watching him. There she was, rooted to the sidewalk, staring. She felt so dumb. Flustered, she turned her head and quickly hurried away.

That afternoon, while her mother fixed supper, Linda sat at the kitchen table with her elbows propped up and her face cradled in her hands. She was staring off into space, thinking about Jimmy.

"Why does school have to be out so soon?" she asked no one in particular.

"I thought you were excited to get out for summer vacation," said her mother.

Linda didn't hear. She was too busy thinking about Jimmy.

"How do you know when you're in love, Mom?" she suddenly asked.

Carolyn stopped stirring. She turned and looked at Linda, who was still staring at the far wall, then laid the spoon down on the stove, took a freshly peeled carrot, and sat down at the table beside her daughter. She broke the carrot in two and slid one half to Linda. "Is there someone at school you like, honey?"

"Yeah," said Linda, taking a bite of her carrot. "His name is Jimmy Stillman. He just moved here from Scranton."

"He must be cute, huh?"

"He's the cutest boy I've ever seen." Linda sighed.

"Cuter than Kenny Williams?"

"A lot cuter than Kenny Williams."

"Is he a good boy?"

Linda nodded. "Real good."

"How do you know?"

"I can just tell. By his eyes."

"I'm anxious to meet this young man."

"Me too," said Linda.

Carolyn leaned back in her chair so Linda couldn't see her smiling.

"I wish school wasn't gonna be out so soon," Linda said again.

In the days that followed, Linda made it a point to get to know Jimmy. She learned that his Grandpa Stillman had died and left his parents the small gray home on Poplar Street, as well as Stillman's Bakery, a moderately successful business on Main Street in Towanda. She also learned that Jimmy had a younger brother named Brad.

It was a sad day for Linda when school let out for the summer. She was certain she wouldn't see Jimmy until September. On two separate occasions during the summer she walked up to Poplar Street, hoping to catch a glimpse of him. She never did. On her third trip she tried to think of what she would say if by chance she did see him. When she couldn't think of anything, she turned around and went back home.

Then one hot day in July, while she was outside riding her bicycle, she saw Jimmy walking down the street in her direction. In one hand he carried a tackle box, and in the other a fishing pole. Linda's throat went dry, and her heart began to pound. Her knees felt so weak that she quit peddling, coasting instead toward Jimmy.

"Hi," she said.

"Hi," said Jimmy.

Linda forgot to put on her brakes and coasted right on past Jimmy. He kept walking, and Linda turned her bike around.

"Where ya goin'?" she asked when she finally caught up with him.

"Fishin'."

That was the end of the conversation. Linda couldn't think of anything else to say, and Jimmy was obviously not in the mood for talking. At a safe distance Linda followed Jimmy to the railroad tracks, where just on the other side he disappeared into the undergrowth and descended the steep bank to the river below.

All the rest of the day Linda watched for him. Just as it got dark she could see him cross the tracks and head in the direction of her house. She ran from the porch and met him under the streetlight.

"Did you catch anything?" she asked breathlessly.

Without a word, Jimmy set his tackle box down in the street and, with great pride, unloaded from his shoulder a stringer of fish. He laid it across the tackle box.

Linda stared at the fish in amazement. "Did you catch all of those?"

"Yep," said Jimmy, standing a little taller than usual.

"What kind are they?"

Pointing, Jimmy said, "The three big ones are small-mouth black bass and the rest are rock bass."

"What are you gonna do with them?" Linda's eyes were still glued to the fish.

"Clean 'em and eat 'em and feed the heads, tails, and guts to the cat."

Linda was speechless. She had never heard of such a horrible thing.

"Gotta go," said Jimmy with a smile. "Cat's waitin'." He gathered up his fish and slung them over his shoulder, picked up the tackle box, and headed down William Street, leaving Linda standing under the streetlight with her jaw still unhinged.

It soon became a ritual. Every morning when Jimmy would walk by, Linda would ask, "Goin' fishin' again?"

Jimmy would always say, "Yep," then head toward the

river. Linda would follow him on her bike to the railroad tracks, where she would watch him descend to the river and its mysteries below. At night, bathed in the soft glow of the streetlight on the corner of Mix Avenue and William Street, Jimmy would display his catch of the day to Linda. These brief moments with him were the highlights of her summer.

One day in early August, when Linda asked, "Goin' fishin'?" Jimmy replied, "Yep. Wanna come?"

Linda swallowed hard and tried not to lose her composure. "I'll have to ask my mother," she said, trying to sound calm. Inside her heart was pounding like a huge kettle drum. She dropped her bike with a clatter and started to run to the house, then caught herself and slowed. When she rounded the corner, out of Jimmy's sight, she ran for all she was worth.

"Mom! Mom!" she cried as she burst through the screen door.

Carolyn rushed into the kitchen, alarmed. "What is it, Linda?"

"Can I go fishin' . . . please?"

Carolyn stopped and put her hands on her hips.

"Fishing? Is that what you're yelling about?"

"Yes—remember the boy I told you about, the one that's cuter than Kenny Williams? His name is Jimmy Stillman and he's so cute and he asked—"

Linda stopped abruptly when she saw her mother look past her to the screen door. A sick feeling washed over her. She slowly turned and followed her mother's gaze.

The morning sun was streaming into the kitchen through the screen door, except where Jimmy was standing with his nose pressed up against the screen. The outline of his body stood out in bold relief. Linda's worst fear was realized—Jimmy had heard everything!

That was how it all began. After that day, Jimmy and

Linda became fishing buddies. Rain, shine, or otherwise, they never missed a day fishing together all that summer. Later that year, when the snow fell and the temperatures dipped below freezing, they even went to Gorman's pond just above Memorial Park to fish through the ice.

The loaded station wagon wove its way through Wysox, Towanda's neighboring town across the river, and started its climb up the hill to the Wyalusing Rocks. Linda turned around to catch one last look at Towanda. She would miss all the trees. There were so many that she had always thought Towanda looked like it was on fire, shrouded with puffs of blue-green smoke. The only visible building was the Bradford County Courthouse with its copper dome shooting up through the green, glistening in the early morning sun. Above the dome the biggest and most beautiful rainbow Linda had ever seen arched over the town. *There'll be nothing like this in California*, she thought as huge tears filled her eyes again and spilled onto her cheeks.

It was true. Towanda was unique—a Huck Finn kind of town, a place most kids only dream about growing up in. Lakes, streams, and creeks were everywhere. In the summer Linda and her family had been able to swim in a different place every day of the week. A place called Big Lamocha was Linda's favorite swimming hole.

In September and October, when the hills and mountains surrounding Towanda were ablaze with autumn colors, all the townspeople would go to Memorial Park on Friday nights to watch the Towanda High Black Knight football team take on the Athens Bulldogs, the Sayre Redskins, or the Wyalusing Rams.

In the winter when it snowed, Linda's father would throw the sleds into the back of the pickup truck and drive to the top of Bridge Street Hill. The kids would sleigh ride three miles to the bottom of the hill, guided by the head-lights of the truck. At the bottom they would throw the sleds back into the truck and drive to the top to start all over again.

Linda wondered if they had lightning bugs in California. It was fun at night to catch them in a jar and then use the jar as a lantern to find her way in the dark. And she would never forget the way a thunderstorm cooled everything off after a hot, humid summer day. It was exciting to sit safe and warm on the front porch swing as the lightning and thunder zipped and crashed all around her. She loved the sound of the rain beating on the roof.

Linda craned her neck and looked out the rear window until she could see Towanda no more. Then she began to sob again.

Glendale, California, was definitely a change from rural northeastern Pennsylvania. Moving from a town of not quite forty-five hundred to the sprawling mass of Los Angeles was a real adjustment for the Mooneys, but although Linda missed Jimmy and Towanda terribly, she was surprised at how quickly she came to like California. There was a sense of excitement and adventure in the balmy air that she couldn't quite describe.

She was amazed at how many palm trees there were. They were everywhere—every size and species. Previously the closest thing she had seen to a palm tree were the leaves a Catholic friend had brought home from church on Palm Sundays in Towanda. Not only that, but orange, grapefruit, and lemon trees now grew right in her own yard. For some reason Linda had never imagined oranges, grapefruit, and lemons growing like apples on trees.

The kumquats that grew on little bushes along the front porch were her favorite thing. Each morning while they were in season Linda would go outside in her pajamas and pop one into her mouth, skin and all. She loved them so much she wanted Jimmy to have some, so she packaged a dozen or so and sent them off to Towanda. They got lost in the mail, and Jimmy didn't receive them for almost two months. When he finally opened the box, he found the little fruits all dried out and shriveled up. He had no idea what they were. He wrote back to Linda, asking if kumquats were to oranges what raisins were to grapes. Linda had to write back and explain.

At first Linda and Jimmy wrote frequently. But as time flew by, the letters and cards became fewer and fewer. Linda had sent the last card on Jimmy's fourteenth birthday. For weeks afterward she checked the mailbox for some kind of reply, but none ever came. She sent another card, thinking that the first had been lost in the mail—but still nothing from Jimmy. Wondering if he had moved, she sent a certified letter. Two weeks later her receipt came back from the postal service signed by Jimmy's mother. She quit writing and never heard from Jimmy again. Before long, Towanda and Jimmy Stillman had become distant and faded memories.

By the time Linda reached sixteen, she no longer looked like the little girl who had spent half of her life traipsing up and down the Susquehanna River chasing crayfish or reeling in carp and suckers from the back of Jimmy Stillman's homemade boat. Tall, tan, blonde, and beautiful, she looked like the consummate "California girl." The years of ballet her mother had insisted upon had given her grace and poise that made her stand out from other girls. Her fun-loving, outgoing personality made her one of the most popular girls at Glendale High, and she was having the time of her life. She adored California—the weather, the shopping, the beach, the boys, and the excitement.

One Saturday early in her junior year, something happened that would forever change her life. Linda had slept in and was fixing herself a late breakfast when through the kitchen window she noticed her father talking to a man and woman down by the gate. The couple were in their late fifties.

"Mother, who are those people Dad's talking to?" she asked.

Carolyn crossed to the window and looked out. "Oh no!" she said. "They're back."

"Who's back?"

"The Jehovah's Witnesses." Carolyn turned from the window. "They were here about a month ago. Your poor father just can't say no to anyone."

"It looks like they're coming in," said Linda, absently taking a bite of her muffin.

"What!" Carolyn, horrified, hurried back to the window. Sure enough, Ted and the couple were coming up the walk toward the house.

"What is your father thinking about? Quick, help me pick up the living room."

In an instant the living room was put in order, and not a second too soon. Just as Linda and Carolyn rushed out of the room, Ted and the couple walked through the front door.

Ted motioned to the couch. "Please have a seat while I get my wife."

He found Carolyn and Linda in the kitchen. Carolyn was standing next to the counter with her arms folded.

"Hi, honey," said Ted. "Come into the living room for a minute. There are some interesting people I want you to meet."

"Ted, I don't want to be a Jehovah's Witness."

"These people aren't Jehovah's Witnesses. They're Mormons."

Linda and Carolyn looked at each other and rolled their eyes.

"That's even worse, Dad," Linda said, trying not to laugh.

"I'm really not interested in doing this, Ted," said Carolyn. "I've got a lot to do. Linda and I are going to run into L.A. and do some shopping."

"C'mon, it'll only take a minute—promise." Ted took Carolyn by the arm and gently pulled her toward the living room.

Carolyn looked at Linda helplessly as she disappeared out of the kitchen. Linda laughed and headed up the back stairs to shower and get ready for the day.

The minute Ted had promised turned into more than two hours. Linda sat in the family room reading a magazine as she waited for the Mormons to leave. When she finally heard them get up she tiptoed into the front hallway to hear what they had to say. As the couple said good-bye at the door, Linda could hear the woman ask, "Have you ever wondered where we came from, why we're here, and where we go after we die?"

"Yes," said Carolyn without hesitation. "All my life."

"Her mother and little brother were killed in a car crash when she was only ten years old," Ted explained.

"How terrible. I'm so sorry," said the woman. "When we return on Monday we will try to answer any questions you've had."

"That would be very interesting," said Carolyn.

Linda couldn't believe what she was hearing. Her parents were having the Mormons come back!

After the couple had gone, Linda went into the living room, where she found her parents doing some pretty heavy thinking. Ted was on the sofa thumbing through a book the Mormons had left, and Carolyn was standing at the window watching the visitors getting into their car.

"'It'll only take a minute,' huh, Dad?" Linda said sarcastically.

Ted looked up from the book, and Carolyn turned from the window.

"Oh, hi, honey," said Ted. "Sorry 'bout that. Actually, I wish you had been here to listen. It was pretty fascinating."

"Did I hear them say they're coming back?"

"Yeah, Monday night. Your mother and I both felt that we should listen to them one more time."

"Ted," Carolyn asked thoughtfully, "did you—did you feel anything when they were here?"

Ted slowly nodded.

Linda thought her parents were acting strangely.

"Are we still going shopping, Mom?" she asked.

Carolyn glanced at her watch. "Oh my goodness, it's one o'clock! Where has the time gone? I'll be ready in ten minutes. Do you want to come with us, honey?" she asked Ted.

"No, I think I'll just stay here. I want to take a look at this book."

A few minutes later, when Linda and Carolyn left to go shopping, Ted was on the sofa reading the book. He didn't even look up to say good-bye. When they got back at six o'clock, he was still on the sofa, buried in the book.

"Must be a great book, huh, Dad?" Linda said as she stood in the entry hall.

Ted just muttered, "Uh-huh," and kept right on reading.

That was the way the rest of the evening went. Ted broke for fifteen minutes to eat and then went back to the book. Linda and her friends went out that night, and when she got home at about one o'clock, Ted and Carolyn were still up talking about their visit with the Mormons. When Linda was ready for bed, she went to her parents' bedroom to say good night. What she saw as she entered made her stop in her tracks. Her parents were on their knees, praying! This was definitely a first. She backed out of the room and waited in the hall until they were finished.

Sunday was more of the same. When Ted wasn't parked on the couch reading the Book of Mormon, he was shadowing Carolyn around the house reading it to her. Sometime around midnight on Sunday, Ted finished the book. Linda and Carolyn were in the family room watching an old Humphrey Bogart movie when Ted walked in. He crossed to Carolyn and handed the book to her.

"It's true," he said softly. They looked at each other for a long moment.

"I'm going to go for a little walk," said Ted. "Be back in a few minutes."

Linda thought she saw tears in her father's eyes. *This is all getting very strange,* she thought to herself. She looked over at her mother, who was no longer watching the television. She was staring intently down at the book.

In bed that night, Linda stared up at the ceiling, considering all that had been going on the past two days. *Some changes are going to happen around here—drastic changes,* she thought. She hadn't mentioned it to her parents, but she kind of wanted to listen to what the Mormons had to say. She too had wondered what this life was all about and where one goes after death. On hot summer days when the fish weren't biting, she and Jimmy used to talk about things like that—especially the summer after Jimmy stumbled upon the woman's body in the Susquehanna. They had decided that there had to be life after death, simply because it was too hard to imagine everything just going black—like a television tube when the TV is turned off.

Linda smiled to herself. *It's funny that I would suddenly think about Jimmy Stillman after so long,* she thought. She turned over in bed and fell asleep still thinking about him.

The Bairds came right on time for their meeting on Monday night. Ted and Carolyn asked Linda and Paul to join them.

Elder and Sister Baird were plain people, farmers from a town in Utah called Payson. They were in the Los Angeles area on what they called a mission for The Church of Jesus Christ of Latter-day Saints—the real name for the Mormon Church. Abner was short and stocky and looked like he had spent too much time in the sun. He was quiet and soft-spoken, with little eyes that shone when he smiled. He had been something called a stake president back in Utah, and he seemed to know the Bible well. His wife, Mary, was slender and tall—at least an inch taller than her husband. She was so friendly and full of life that Linda liked her immediately. The house seemed warmer and happier when the Bairds were there. All the family could feel it.

The first thing the Bairds did was show a video called "Man's Search For Happiness." When it was over, Ted and Carolyn had tears in their eyes. Linda and Paul had to admit to themselves that they were touched.

The visitors spent the rest of the evening talking about what they called the plan of salvation. Mary began by talking about the preexistence, a place where she said everyone lived before this life. She told them that life on earth was a time for everyone to prepare to meet God by showing him that they could keep his commandments. After a person dies, Mary told them, he goes to the spirit world. He is judged according to his works.

As Linda listened, she thought to herself, *I believe this— it's true!* She glanced at Paul. He seemed to be very interested.

The missionaries talked about Joseph Smith and the restoration of the church that Jesus Christ had organized when he was on the earth, which they said had subsequently apostatized from the truth. Abner spoke of baptism and the authority to baptize. At the close of the discussion he looked at Ted and asked, "If you knew that what we have told you tonight is true, would you be baptized into The Church of Jesus Christ of Latter-day Saints?"

"Yes," said Ted, without the least bit of hesitation.

Linda and Paul jerked their heads toward their father. They were startled by his direct answer.

"Carolyn," asked Abner, "if you knew these things were true, would you be baptized into The Church of Jesus Christ of Latter-day Saints?"

"Yes," said Carolyn. She looked at Ted, and they shared a smile.

Paul and Linda looked at each other.

"Paul," said Abner, "if you knew it was true, would you be baptized?"

"If I knew it was true."

"And how about you, Linda?" Mary asked with a smile.

"Yes," said Linda, nodding her head.

Abner set the baptismal date for three weeks from the following Saturday. He promised them they would know that the Church was true if they would read the Book of Mormon daily and pray to know that it was true. He also counseled them to pray to know whether Joseph Smith was a prophet. The family agreed to attend church that Sunday.

Linda was right about changes coming into her family. They began praying individually and as a family that very night. The following Sunday they attended the Glendale Third Ward.

Abner and Mary had primed the entire ward to watch for and welcome the Mooneys. When they arrived home from church on that first Sunday, their hands and arms were tired from shaking so many hands. They were impressed. On the exact date originally appointed by the Bairds, the Mooneys were baptized and confirmed members of the Church.

It didn't take long before the family became an integrated part of the ward. Within the year Ted was ordained an elder, and a short time later he was called to be a counselor in the elders quorum presidency. Carolyn was called to teach in Primary and spent hours each week preparing for her lessons. Paul attended the institute at UCLA and began having serious thoughts about going on a mission. Linda quickly made friends with the rest of the Laurels and youth.

Linda's junior year at Glendale High was eventful as well. She was chosen junior prom queen and was a member of the cheerleading squad. Her senior year promised to be every bit as exciting.

But Linda was soon to learn that for her there would be no senior year at Glendale High.

# 4

It was the last week in July. Linda had spent a day at Santa Monica Beach with her friends. When she arrived home she found her mother running about half-dressed, getting ready for a dinner engagement.

"Hurry," she said, "your father will be here any minute. He's taking us to dinner. He has something very important to tell us—I think he got a promotion. Paul's going to meet us at the restaurant."

"What restaurant?" Linda asked, slipping out of her clothes.

"I think he said the Grotto."

"If it's the Grotto, it's a promotion."

Within the hour the whole family was seated at the Grotto, Glendale's finest and most expensive seafood restaurant. Every wall, including the entire floor, was a giant aquarium filled with an array of spectacular, brilliantly colored tropical fish.

"Look, the wallpaper and the rug are moving!" said Paul. "How do they do that?"

"Shhh," Linda hushed him. "This is a classy place."

"Then what are you doing here?" kidded Paul.

A waiter in a tuxedo brought the menus. Linda opened hers and began reading. The prices were unbelievable— one hundred and fifty dollars for lobster tail! In parentheses just below the entry it read, "We finance; loan applications available." A simple shrimp salad was thirty dollars.

Paul looked up at his father. "I've got an idea, Dad," he said. "Let's go to Skippers instead, and with the money we save you can buy me that convertible I've been looking at."

"The prices are a little steep, honey," said Carolyn. "It wouldn't bother me a bit if we ate someplace else."

"Relax," said Ted. "Take a look at the specials. They aren't so bad."

All eyes went to the specials, which were printed on a piece of paper and clipped to the inside of the menu. As Linda read the first entree on the list, her eyes grew big and her jaw dropped. Her resemblance to the sea bass swimming just below her feet was uncanny.

The first entree read "Susquehanna Smallmouth Black Bass, caught by Jimmy Stillman and flown in fresh from Towanda, Pennsylvania." Linda's eyes jumped to the next entrees—"James Street Rock Bass, Towanda's finest," "Gorman Pond's Best Bluegill," "William Street Walleyed Pike." Every single entree on the list in some way or other referred to Towanda or its surrounding areas. Linda, Carolyn, and Paul looked up incredulously at Ted, who was leaning back in his chair, laughing.

"What's going on, Dad?" demanded Linda. "What is all this about?"

When Ted quit laughing, he sat forward and spoke. "I've been asked by the company to head up the plant in Towanda. They want us there before September."

The table went deathly quiet. After a long moment, Carolyn finally broke the silence. "What did you tell them?"

"I told them I'd have to talk to my family and that I'd get back with them no later than Monday."

"What kind of money are they talking, Dad?" asked Paul.

"Let me put it this way: If we decide we want to go back to Pennsylvania, we can all order the lobster tail. If we stay here in Glendale, we sneak out one at a time and go to Skippers."

"I'll have the lobster tail," said Paul.

Linda shot a disgusted look at Paul *Here he is, in his second year of college, and he's still as dumb as ever,* she thought. But what did he care. He was out of the house, living near the university. She still had another year left in high school, and her senior year promised to be her best yet.

Linda turned from Paul and looked at her mother. Carolyn reached over and squeezed Ted's hand. She was beaming. Linda suddenly felt sick and sank back slowly in her chair.

"Anybody here want to meet me at Skippers?" she said. But she spoke so quietly that no one heard.

At one o'clock that Saturday afternoon, Linda and the family began fasting and praying for guidance. Secretly she hoped the answer would be no, that they shouldn't move. But for some reason, she knew that the answer would be yes.

Late that night, heavy clouds began rolling in off the ocean, darkening the skies over Glendale. Linda crawled out of her bedroom window in her pajamas and sat on the porch roof, where she could see the storm moving in her direction. Daggers of bright lightning lit the far sky, followed by cannon bursts of thunder that trailed off in the distance.

A cool breeze carrying the sweet scent of the impending rain suddenly blew through Linda's hair and made her think of Towanda. Whenever it rained Linda thought of Towanda. But as beautiful as Towanda was, she didn't want to go back. California was where she wanted to stay. *I could stay with one of my friends in the ward,* she told herself. *I could graduate here, then spend the summer with my parents before going to college.*

She lay back on the warm roof, wondering how to break the new idea to her parents. But as she thought about spending a year away from her family, she began to feel lonesome. Since joining the Church she had felt closer than ever to Paul and her parents. The idea of being a forever family felt good and right. If she stayed behind and they went off to Pennsylvania without her, they wouldn't be a complete family—at least, not for a while. Whatever the family decided, Linda knew they had to stick together.

She closed her eyes and prayed, and as she did she could feel the cool, wet drops of rain falling softly on her face. The rain began to fall harder. The wetter Linda became, the faster she prayed. She quickly ended with one last "Should we move to Pennsylvania? In the name of Jesus Christ, amen." On her "amen," a tremendous bolt of lightning scorched the night sky, illuminating the land for miles. It was so bright that Linda could see it through her closed eyelids.

Then, without warning, thunder exploded furiously overhead, making the whole house seem to shudder. Linda screamed with fright and scrambled from the roof, through the opened window, and into her bedroom. She dived into her bed and hid beneath the covers, feeling as though she were five years old again as she lay there listening to the thunder.

A silly thought entered her mind: Could the thunder have been her answer to the question "Should we move back to Towanda?" *It did sound like a definite no,* she told herself. The thought made her smile for the first time since hearing that her family might leave California. But she knew she was only kidding herself. The answer she was waiting faithfully for would come in the form of an impression in her mind and heart that would leave absolutely no doubt what she should do.

Her stomach suddenly growled with hunger, and for a split second Linda thought it was the funniest thunder she had ever heard. When she realized that she was hungry from fasting, it made her think of her seminary teacher, Brother McCallister. "Fasting without prayer is just plain starving," he would always say. Linda poked her head out of the covers and slid out of bed to her knees to offer one last prayer before going to sleep.

Sunday was wet and foggy. Before breaking her fast that afternoon, Linda drove to the top of Glendale Canyon, where she could be alone and offer her last prayer from that secluded place. This was one of her favorite spots, and it was where she usually went when she wanted to get away and be by herself. From here she could usually see all the way to Los Angeles and beyond, but today the thick fog prevented her from seeing a thing. She looked up at the sky where the fog was melting away, revealing a faint blue. Momentarily the sun would break through, and it would be a beautiful day.

Linda turned off the ignition. She felt different today—her mind was clear, and her heart was right. She knew it was because of the fast. Her desires were less definite. She wanted to know what the Lord had in mind for her. She would put her trust in him, and she knew she would receive her answer.

She bowed her head and began to pray, and the words came easily. Overhead the sun burned through the fog and bathed the canyon with a warm glow. When Linda finished, she looked up and gasped. Her eyes grew big as she gripped the steering wheel and stared out through the windshield at the scene below her. A thick river of fog filled the canyon below. It seemed to be flowing as it meandered to the bottom of the canyon. The sun had finally broken through the clouds and fog, and its rays were reflecting off the golden dome of the old Glendale city building. A huge, glorious rainbow arched over all of Glendale. It was nearly the same scene she had witnessed on her way out of Towanda six years ago.

Tears filled her eyes as an indescribable warmth filled her heart. She was in Towanda, not Glendale, and it felt good and right. She started the car and headed for home.

# 5

It was late in the afternoon when Linda and her mother flew into the Scranton airport. They rented a car, then drove the sixty-eight miles to Towanda. Linda was silent most of the way. Although she knew in her heart that this move was meant to be, it was hard to leave California. But it was only a year before she would be off to BYU, where she would be reunited with the friends she had grown to love in the Glendale ward. She could put up with almost anything for a year, she thought to herself—even being the new kid in Towanda.

Linda and Carolyn were anxious to see Ted again. He had gone on to Towanda ahead of them to find a house and get situated in his business. Paul was still at UCLA and would join them at Christmas.

Just as they were about to make their final descent into Towanda, Carolyn slowed the car and pulled off the road into a popular tourist lookout area. "This has always been one of my favorite spots," said Carolyn. "Let's take a look."

They got out of the car and climbed to a point where they could see the Susquehanna River nearly two thousand feet directly below them, flowing for miles and miles through the beautiful blue-green forests and farmlands. They stared in silent awe.

"Isn't that the most beautiful sight you have ever seen?" Carolyn exclaimed.

Linda just nodded.

The setting sun filtering through the trees on the hills and along the banks of the river created a dazzling, shimmering effect on the black water. Linda leaned forward on the rail and looked down at the river. There in the half-light she could see a small boat anchored near the middle of the river. In the tiny boat was a lone fisherman. For the first time in a long while Linda thought of Jimmy Stillman. As silly as it seemed, she could feel her heart beat just a little faster. *What does he look like now?* she wondered. *Will we be friends again? Or will time have changed everything?* A strange, almost mystical feeling came over her, pressing and urging her to hurry on to Towanda.

"Let's go, Mom," she said, straightening up. "Dad's gonna be waiting for us."

They took one last look and hurried to the car.

On the river below, just as the sun disappeared over the horizon, Jimmy Stillman pulled his lead anchor from the dark waters and laid it on the wooden floor of his tiny boat. He grabbed an oar in each hand and, with powerful strokes, rowed effortlessly to shore.

# 6

It was dark when Linda and her mother pulled into the driveway of their new home on Chestnut Street. As the headlights bathed the house they could see Ted sitting on the front porch swing. He jumped to his feet and rushed down the porch stairs to the car, and Carolyn and Linda hurried out to meet him.

"Welcome back to Towanda!" said Ted as he took them both into his arms. "How do you like the house?"

Linda and Carolyn stepped back and looked up.

"Oh, Ted!" Carolyn exclaimed. "It's even more beautiful than the pictures you sent."

"Wait'll you see the inside," said Ted.

"It's big, Dad," said Linda, laughing. "Real big."

The house was a large, one-hundred-year-old clapboard Victorian with a three-story turret and a gigantic front porch that wrapped around the whole front of the house. Three giant maples, a walnut, and two chestnut trees shaded the front and side yards. It was one of the nicest homes in Towanda.

"Hungry?" asked Ted.

"Starved," said Linda.

"C'mon, I've got something for you inside." He put an arm around each of them and guided them up the stairs and onto the porch, where he turned and said, "Listen . . . it's been like that all night."

Linda and Carolyn listened.

"What, Dad? I don't hear a thing," said Linda.

"I don't hear anything, either," said Carolyn. "Just the wind through the trees."

"And the sound of crickets," added Linda.

"That's right," said Ted. "No police sirens, no traffic, nothing. Just the sound of the wind through the trees—and crickets. It's good to be back, isn't it?"

He smiled contentedly as he guided them inside.

The next morning, warm rays of sunlight filtered in through the window shades in Linda's room and washed across the floor onto her bed. Birds chirping and a noisy squirrel chattering outside awakened her, and she slid out of bed and padded to the window. A fat gray squirrel was perched on a branch of the walnut tree, clutching a walnut. He eyed Linda for a moment, then jumped to another branch and scampered away.

Linda got dressed and went downstairs to the kitchen, where she fixed herself a bowl of cold cereal. She stepped out onto the porch and sat on the swing. As she swung and ate her cereal she thought how funny it was that she was living on Chestnut Street. Chestnut had always been her favorite street in all of Towanda. On her way home from school each day she would purposely go out of her way several blocks to walk along it. The street and houses were just as she had remembered—large horse chestnut trees with trunks she could never reach her arms around still flanked the pavement in front of the oldest and best-kept homes in the town. She could still remember gathering bouquets of horse chestnut blossoms and selling them to kind and amused neighbors. When the horse chestnuts fell, she and her friends would carve holes in them to make rings and necklaces. The home she was now living in had always been her favorite. Knowing that at last she was going to live in her favorite house on her favorite street made the move from California a little bit easier.

Linda was showered and dressed and on her way out the door when her parents got up.

"Where are you going, Linda?" Carolyn asked.

"I thought I'd go for a walk—see what's changed and what hasn't. I won't be long."

"Try and get back by noon, and I'll have lunch for you."

"Okay," said Linda as she stepped out onto the porch.

She set out down Chestnut Street and crossed over to Third Street and the Third Street bridge. Halfway across the bridge, she paused and looked over the iron rail and down at Plank Road. It was at least fifty feet to the bottom. The old tar-paper shanties that had once littered the old road were gone, replaced by new apartment buildings. As Linda looked down, a smile spread across her face at the vivid recollection of an incident that had taken place right on that very spot.

It had been the most exciting and unforgettable Halloween night of her life. She and Jimmy were on their way to do some serious trick-or-treating on Chestnut Street when they came across the Larkin brothers, two of the rowdiest kids in Towanda. These boys were lugging a huge pumpkin that they had no doubt stolen from some- body's porch, and they carried it to the center of the bridge, where they waited for a car to come up Plank Road. As the two of them hoisted the jack-o-lantern to the rail, they spotted Jimmy and Linda.

"Say a word and you're dead," threatened the older of the Larkin brothers.

Linda and Jimmy froze in their tracks.

"C'mon, Jimmy, let's get outta here," Linda whispered.

"Are you kiddin'?" Jimmy sported a huge grin. "I wanna see this."

All of a sudden, headlights could be seen turning off Main Street and heading up Plank Road.

"On three," said the older brother.

As the headlights got closer, Linda could feel her heart beginning to pound. Jimmy stepped close to the rail and gripped it tightly. Their eyes grew larger and larger as the car below got closer and closer.

"One—two—" said the older brother. "Three!"

"TRICK OR TREAT!" screamed the younger boy.

Linda gasped as the huge orange bomb was released, disappearing into the dark with an eerie whoosh. Linda, Jimmy, and the Larkins leaned over the rail bug-eyed, holding their breath.

Several seconds seemed to go by, and then it happened—KABOOM! The pumpkin hit the hood of the car dead center, exploding on impact. The noise it made was so loud that everyone who lived on Plank Road came running out of their houses, expecting to see a head-on collision and people strewn all over the road.

Linda turned to look at the Larkins, but they were nearly at the end of the bridge, running for their lives.

"C'mon," said Jimmy, "we gotta get outta here!"

An old woman below looked up and saw the silhouettes of Jimmy and Linda. "You up there!" she began screaming hysterically. "Stop!"

Several men spotted them and jumped into their cars.

Linda was frozen with fear, unable to move.

"C'mon, Linda!" shouted Jimmy. He grabbed her by the coat and pulled her away from the rail. They ran and ran until they thought their hearts and lungs would burst.

All that night there was a manhunt for the kids who had thrown the pumpkin off the bridge. The following day the local newspaper carried a picture of the damaged car on the front page. The crater in the hood where the pumpkin had landed was enormous. A reward of one hundred dollars was offered by the police for any information on who may have dropped the pumpkin, and at school everybody was talking about the Third Street bridge pumpkin caper. Jimmy and Linda never breathed a word to anyone about what they knew.

Linda walked off the bridge and headed for Poplar Street, where she had last seen Jimmy Stillman. As she approached the house she could hear the sound of a lawn mower engine coming from the backyard.

*That must be Jimmy!* The thought brought her to a standstill. She could feel her heart beating faster. *This is ridiculous,* she told herself, and moved toward the gate that led into the backyard.

A teenage boy burst through the gate, pushing a lawn mower. Linda's heart jumped. The boy was Linda's age. He was short and skinny. His dark brown hair was clipped short and worn in a flattop.

Linda was sick with disappointment. This wasn't the way Jimmy was supposed to turn out. She braced herself as the boy pushed the lawn mower in her direction. A few feet from Linda he looked up and noticed her. It was more than obvious that he thought Linda was a knockout. He smiled, then reached down and cut the engine.

"Hi," said Linda, managing to smile back.

"Hi." The boy flashed a cheesy grin and moved closer.

"Jimmy?"

"If it's Jimmy you want, I'll be Jimmy. How can I be of service?"

This wasn't Jimmy! Linda was so relieved she wanted to hug him.

Linda learned that the boy's name was Dillan Bayfield. He was a junior at Towanda High School. The name Stillman sounded familiar to him, but the family no longer lived in this house. An old couple from New Jersey had purchased it three years ago, and he took care of the lawn for them during the summer.

Dillan Bayfield was the most persistent boy Linda had ever met. He told her that if she didn't at least give him her phone number he would walk with her all the way home and ask her mother for it. After he got the number he walked two and a half blocks down Poplar Street before he finally said good-bye. Whether she liked it or not, Linda had a friend for life in Dillan Bayfield.

After her twentieth good-bye to Dillan she headed down Poplar Street toward the Towanda business district, wondering about Jimmy. Where was he? What if he no longer lived in Towanda? What if he and his family had moved to another state? It really didn't matter, Linda tried to tell herself, because in just one short year she'd be off to BYU. But she couldn't help it—the thought that Jimmy might not be in Towanda anymore left her feeling empty inside.

Linda took a stroll down Towanda's Main Street. Nothing had really changed—the shopping was still atrocious. She started getting withdrawal pains, remembering how wonderful the stores were in California. When her dad and brother went on ward fathers-and-sons outings, Linda and Carolyn would take off and spend the day in the garment district of L.A. hunting bargains. It was glorious. Thank goodness cities like Scranton and Elmira were only an hour away, and if things got really desperate, it would take just four hours to get to New York City.

When it got close to noon Linda decided to head for home. She took the long route down River Street so she could gaze out at the river as she walked. When she passed the old telephone company building and parking lot she paused, wondering if the path she and Jimmy used to take to get down to the river was still there. She decided to cross the railroad tracks to see if she could find it.

It was as though she had never left—she found the path instantly and followed it down to the river's edge. At the bottom was a small, shady place the locals called Hunsinger's Cove after the old man who lived in the house across the street. Fishermen kept their boats here, tied to trees and rocks. It was from this spot that Jimmy and Linda had launched on their first journey to the island.

The boat! Why hadn't Linda thought of that before? If the boat was here, that would mean Jimmy was too. A sudden rush of excitement shot through her as she scanned the cove. But there was no sign of it.

The empty feeling returned, and Linda turned to go back up the path when something caught her eye. At the far end of the cove, partially concealed behind a larger boat, was a smaller one that looked like it might be Jimmy's. Linda hurried across the rocks to where the old boat rocked gently in the water. One look, and Linda knew it was Jimmy's boat. He was here!

She sat down on a large rock and stared at the boat, and as a slide show of memories flashed in her mind, something on the side of the boat both startled and touched her at the same time.

She covered her mouth with a trembling hand and leaned forward. Tears glistened in her eyes. There, on the bow of the little boat, were the unmistakable words *The Linda*, painted with the unsure, unsteady, yet careful strokes of a young boy. Although the years had caused the paint to crack and fade, Jimmy's original intent was still clear—to hang on to the memory of Linda.

Linda slid off the rock with one last look at the boat before hurrying home to give her mother a report on her findings that morning. The mile walk back home to Chestnut Street seemed a short jaunt. For the first time, Linda was happy to be back in Towanda.

# 7

That Sunday Linda and her mother were able to meet their new brothers and sisters of the Towanda Ward. During Sunday School Linda was introduced to two girls who were close to her age—Allison Turner and Beth Whitehead. Allison would be a senior like Linda, and Beth would be a junior. Linda was glad that she wasn't going to be the only Mormon in her class. The three girls became fast friends and vowed to stick together.

The small ward was undergoing a major transition. Bishop Reeves, who had served four years, was being transferred to Norway by his company. It was an emotional fast-and-testimony meeting, with members filing to the pulpit to express their love for the bishop, his counselors, and their families. No one seemed to care that the meeting went forty-five minutes past the allotted time. At the close of the meeting, the announcement was made that a new bishop would be called and ready to serve the following Sunday.

Carolyn and Ted turned and looked at each other, and as they did, the sweet spirit emanating from the Holy Ghost touched them both. They felt strongly that Ted would be the ward's new bishop. Tears filled their eyes, and Ted took Carolyn's hand in his.

Linda noticed her parents crying. *It's strange that they already seem so attached to the ward and the bishop,* she thought.

As Ted shared the special experience with Linda at the dinner table that day, the phone rang. Linda hurried into the kitchen and answered it.

"Hello? . . . Yes, he is. May I ask who's calling?"

When Linda returned to the dining room, she had a very sober look on her face. "It's for you, Dad. It's the stake president."

Ted looked at Carolyn with raised eyebrows. Without saying a word, he was asking her, "Can I do this? Will you help me?"

Carolyn gave Ted a nod and a reassuring smile. With that he pushed away from the table and went into the kitchen, with Carolyn and Linda following.

"I've been expecting your call, president," said Ted. "What time would you like us to meet with you?"

After Ted hung up the phone, he looked at Carolyn. "The stake president wants us to meet with him at the chapel as soon as we can get there." A hush came over the room. Ted reached out and took Carolyn and Linda in his arms.

That afternoon Ted humbly and willingly accepted the call to be the new bishop. The following Sunday the ward unanimously sustained him, and after church the stake president ordained him to his new calling. Linda was especially reflective because of something that had happened as she listened to President Andrus's words as he gave her father a blessing. *"You are here on an errand of the Lord—not just you, Brother Mooney, but also members of your family. Wounded hearts are in your midst that only you and members of your family can heal. Many souls will be brought unto Christ because you have heeded his call to come to this place."*

The words were indelibly impressed upon Linda's mind, because as the Spirit dictated the words *"wounded hearts are in your midst,"* something peculiar happened. The image of Jimmy Stillman flashed in her mind. Without even trying she had thought of him. He was standing in the river, looking at her. And he was young, the way she still remembered him. That was all.

As the car turned on Chestnut Street, a happy feeling came over Linda. School was starting the next day, and she was glad.

# 8

Linda awoke extra early to get ready for her first day at school. At seven-thirty sharp she picked up Allison and headed for the high school. As she and Allison exited the car and walked through the school parking lot, no one seemed to remember or recognize her, for she was no longer a skinny, gangly eleven-year-old with glasses.

As she walked to the main office to register, she searched the face of every boy she saw, looking for Jimmy Stillman. Then, with her new schedule in hand, she went to her first period history class. Twice the teacher had to stop his lecture to get the boys to settle down and pay attention to him instead of the new student. It was embarrassing, but Linda wouldn't have missed it for anything.

Just before chemistry class Linda took her schedule to the front of the room, where her teacher, Mr. Campbell, was seated at his desk. Campbell welcomed her and wrote her name in his roll book. As he wrote, Linda moved closer and glanced at the names, hoping to see Jimmy among them. *Smith . . . Stuart . . .Stillman!* There it was—*James Stillman.* He was in this class! In fact, he was probably sitting in the classroom at that very moment, watching her. The thought made her feel flustered.

"Linda, take a seat anywhere," said Campbell. "I'll have a seating chart made up in a few days."

"Thank you," said Linda. She walked slowly toward a vacant seat in the fourth row, scanning the room for Jimmy. This wasn't easy because each boy she looked at was looking right back at her. She took her seat, then casually looked to her right, then to her left, studying the face of each boy. None of them looked the way she remembered Jimmy.

Just after the second bell rang for class to begin, Mr. Campbell started to take roll. "Jim Abbott, Greg Ault" . . .

Linda continued looking for Jimmy.

"Leslie Lewis, Sherry Lowder . . . "

Suddenly the door of the room opened, and a well-built young man with dark brown hair and soft brown eyes stepped in and closed the door. Linda turned and watched as he moved to the nearest vacant seat and sat down.

*No way could this be Jimmy Stillman,* Linda thought to herself. This boy was at least six feet two. Jimmy had always been shorter than she was. She still could remember how he would walk on the railroad tracks so that he could be just as tall as she was.

"Joe Rosenbaum," continued Mr. Campbell.

*Jimmy was a skinny little kid. No way could he grow into something like this,* Linda reasoned. There was no getting around it; this guy was buff. He was built like some of the lifeguards at Santa Monica Beach—broad at the shoulders and narrow at the hips.

Alana Sloan was the next name Mr. Campbell read from the roll. Linda looked more closely at the boy, wishing he would look in her direction. If he did, she would know immediately if it was Jimmy. But this couldn't be him—

"James Stillman," said Mr. Campbell.

Linda's heart stopped. She stared at the boy, wondering if he would answer.

"Yeah," said the boy in a deep, masculine voice.

"Let's not make a habit of being late, Jim," said Campbell.

Jimmy only nodded. Linda knew she was staring, but she didn't care. This was her buddy, Jimmy Stillman! She couldn't believe how big he had grown and how handsome he was. She was incredulous.

"Jody Wheeler . . . Kurt Young." Campbell was finished with the roll. He stood up from his desk, looked at Linda, and smiled. "Students, we have a new student who just moved back to Towanda from California. I'd like you to welcome Linda Mooney."

Jimmy jerked his head toward Linda. Linda slowly looked from Mr. Campbell to Jimmy. He was staring at her. Their eyes met and held for a long moment. She smiled and gave him a little finger wave. Jimmy reciprocated with a half smile and nodded, and then his expression seemed to cloud as he turned away and pretended to study his new textbook. He didn't look at her the rest of the period.

Linda was confused—it was almost like he wished she wasn't there. When the bell rang he was the first one out the door. Linda hurried out of the classroom, thinking that he would be waiting for her in the hall. But he wasn't.

*Something's wrong,* she thought, hurt. *This isn't the Jimmy Stillman I remember.* She vowed to herself that the next time she saw him she would give him a piece of her mind.

In a small school news circulates at the speed of light. By the next morning word was out that a "fox" from California had infiltrated Towanda High. Linda had only been at the school for a few hours, and she was already one of the most popular girls on campus.

The next day Jimmy was late again for chemistry and the first one out the door when the bell rang. Linda made an attempt to catch up with him, but it was futile. At lunchtime Linda, Allison, and Beth Whitehead drove to Pudgies Drive-in in north Towanda, followed by a procession of at least ten cars, packed with hopeful boys. Allison and Beth were having the time of their lives.

Just as Linda was about to bite into a burger, Allison screeched, "Don't look now, but the cutest guy in the whole county is in the Jeep right next to our car, staring at us."

"Let's try that again," said Beth. "He's not staring at us, he's staring at Linda."

"Who is he?" asked Linda casually, looking straight ahead.

"Beau Taylor," Allison answered. "He's the first-string quarterback. He moved here two years ago from Boston."

"Most girls would kill just to be seen with him," said Beth.

Linda turned to get a good look at this Beau Taylor. He was right across from her. Their eyes met, and they shared a smile. *He's cute,* Linda thought to herself, *but he doesn't even come close to Jimmy Stillman.* She turned back and dipped a fry in her sauce. "He's kinda cute," she said.

"*Kinda* cute?" Allison was insulted. "Gimme a break. He's gorgeous, and you know it."

Just then, something in Linda's rearview mirror caught her eye. It was an old, beat-up Ford pickup pulling off the road into the drive-in, and Jimmy Stillman was behind the wheel. Linda watched until she could no longer see him in her mirror, then turned her head to see where he was going to park. He had pulled in three cars away from the Jeep Beau Taylor was sitting in. Beau Taylor thought she was looking at him and shot Linda his best smile.

"I'll be right back, guys," said Linda to Allison and Beth.

Her timing couldn't have been any better, for just as Beau Taylor decided to make his move and slide out of the

Jeep, Linda opened her door to get out. The edge of the door caught Beau right on the front of his kneecap. He was in pain, but he hid it well.

"Oh, I'm sorry," Linda exclaimed. "Are you all right?"

"Yeah . . . sure." Beau tried hard not to grimace.

"I'm glad," said Linda as she hurried past him to get to Jimmy's truck.

Beau Taylor *was* hurt. At the game with Wyalusing later that night, he would reinjure the same knee in the first quarter and be sidelined for the rest of the game. Towanda would eventually lose by only one point. Linda was having a greater impact on Towanda than she could ever imagine.

Jimmy Stillman was ordering lunch when Linda opened his door and slid in. He turned and looked at her.

"What's up?" was the only thing he could think of to say, but just as soon as he said it he knew it was dumb. Linda was upset, but not half as much as she was pretending to be. She was an actress at heart. She had learned early that pretending to be more upset than she really was did wonders with boys.

" 'What's up?' You haven't seen me for six years, and all you have to say is 'What's up?' C'mon, Jimmy, you can do better than that. And why have you been avoiding me like the plague?"

"I haven't been avoiding you," said Jimmy. "I've just been—in a hurry lately, that's all."

For some reason, Linda didn't care that he was lying. She was enjoying herself. She was with Jimmy Stillman again, and it felt good.

Jimmy took a long look at Linda. "You've changed. If Campbell hadn't said your name, I never would have recognized you."

"And what's that supposed to mean?" She teased, knowing darn well what it meant.

"It means you're lookin' good." Jimmy was a little embarrassed. He laughed, and his eyes twinkled and crinkled at the corners.

*His eyes are still the color of horse chestnuts,* Linda thought to herself. She loved his voice; it was so deep and masculine. She wished he would talk more so she could listen to it.

"Still singing soprano with the boy's choir?" she asked.

"Right." Jimmy smiled.

Jimmy's take-out order arrived. He paid for it and set it on the seat between them. "So what's it like being back?"

"Fun. I miss California, but I'm having a good time."

There was another pause.

"Still king of the river?" Linda turned the conversation back to Jimmy.

Jimmy remembered and smiled.

"Still doing a lot of fishing?" she asked.

"Not as much as I'd like to. But I still get out once in awhile."

"How 'bout taking me with you sometime? I haven't been fishing since I left."

Jimmy nodded. "Yeah, sure."

"How 'bout Saturday?"

"I'll have to check my work schedule. I'll let you know."

"How's your family?"

Jimmy paused for a moment. "They're okay."

Linda wished she hadn't asked, because Jimmy suddenly grew quiet.

There was a long pause; then he spoke. "Gotta run."

Linda glanced at her watch. "School doesn't start for another half hour."

"I know, but I gotta get to work. My boss is going to a funeral, and I told him I'd fill in for him." Jimmy grabbed the key and was ready to turn it. "Good seeing you, Linda."

She knew that was her cue to get out of the truck. "You're gonna call me on the fishing, right?"

Jimmy turned the key and fired the engine. "Yeah, soon as I look at the schedule."

Linda opened the door and slid out. "See ya tomorrow."

"Okay."

Linda closed the door. She watched until Jimmy's pickup reached the road and raced back in the direction of town. *Why did he turn so cold at the mention of his family?* she wondered. She turned and walked slowly back to her car.

The next day and the day after, Jimmy didn't show up for chemistry class. In fact, he didn't show up for any of his classes. Linda decided to find out why.

After school on Thursday she stopped at the Towanda Bakery to visit Jimmy's parents. As she entered she was greeted by the familiar smell of baking bread. She and Jimmy used to come in here after school before going fishing and snitch a doughnut or two, then run out before Jimmy's parents could put them to work.

As the door closed behind Linda, a girl in her twenties emerged from the back of the store.

"May I help you?" she said.

"Yes—is Mr. or Mrs. Stillman here?"

A confused look came over the girl's face. "Mrs. Stillman is here. I'll get her."

A moment later Mrs. Stillman came out front. Her face and apron were covered with flour. Linda hardly recognized her—she seemed much older, and her brown eyes had lost the vibrant glow that Linda remembered.

She smiled cordially at Linda. "May I help you?"

"Hello, Mrs. Stillman. It's me—Linda Mooney. My family and I just moved back from California."

Mrs. Stillman's eyes lit up, and a smile warmed her face. "Linda! How are you? I'd give you a hug, but I'd get flour all over you." She grasped Linda by the shoulders and stepped back. "Look how you've grown up. You're beautiful! Does Jimmy know you're here?"

"Yes, we have a chemistry class together."

Mrs. Stillman looked puzzled. "That's funny. Jimmy never even mentioned it. But then, we don't get to see each other much these days, with school and both of us working."

Linda felt sick inside. So Jimmy hadn't even told his mother. But the actress in her kept her right on smiling.

"How's the rest of the family?" she asked.

Mrs. Stillman quit smiling. She stood straighter and took a deep breath. "Of course you wouldn't know— you've been gone," she said. "Little Brad was killed in an accident about three years ago. Not long after that Jack and I got divorced. It's just Jimmy and me now."

Linda was shocked. "I had no idea. I'm so sorry, Mrs. Stillman."

"It was a terrible time in our lives, but whether you want it to or not, life goes on, doesn't it?" She laughed wearily. "Oh, I'm so glad to see you, Linda. And I'm sure Jimmy is thrilled that you're back. Brad's death and the divorce were hard on him. He was only fourteen, you know. He keeps to himself a lot these days and doesn't have many friends. Maybe you can help bring him out."

When Linda left the bakery she was covered with flour—she hadn't been able to leave without hugging Mrs. Stillman. She cried all the way home.

The next morning Jimmy was late again for chemistry. Linda knew that as soon as the closing bell rang he would be out the door before she could speak to him, so she scribbled a little note, folded it, and passed it to the girl in the next row.

"Would you please pass this to Jimmy Stillman," she whispered. The girl passed the note to the boy across from her with the same instructions.

Mr. Campbell looked up at just the right moment and saw the last exchange. He moved down the aisle and intercepted the note just before it got to Jimmy.

"All right, who's responsible for the note?"

Linda could feel her face growing hotter by the second. She slowly raised her hand.

"The rule is, any note confiscated by me in this class is community property. What do you say, class—shall we read it?"

The class whooped, hollered, and applauded. It was unanimous.

Campbell slowly unfolded the note. He read it first to himself, to the protests of some of the boys. With raised eyebrows he looked first at Linda, then at Jimmy. "Very interesting."

"C'mon, read it," shouted someone from the back of the room.

Campbell held the note in front of him and read, "Dear Jimmy—how about Saturday at six? We can meet at Hunsingers Cove. I'll bring . . . the bait. Linda."

The class went crazy.

Linda, red-faced, was laughing and trying to explain. "Fishing, I meant fishing!"

Campbell tossed the note onto Jimmy's desk. "Sounds like an offer you can't refuse."

Jimmy looked straight ahead and half smiled.

When the bell rang, Jimmy got up and walked out the door. Linda sprang to her feet and hurried after him. Little did she know that he was waiting for her in the hall right outside the door, and when she came running out she almost mowed him down.

"What are you doing?" she asked.

"Waiting for you."

"Oh. . . . I'm so embarrassed. I can't believe he read the note."

There was a pause, then Jimmy spoke. "I can't go fishing Saturday. Gotta work all day."

"Can't you get out of it?"

Jimmy shook his head. "No, my boss is counting on me." His eyes didn't meet her gaze. "What's your next class?"

"English."

"You'd better be going or you're gonna be late."

Linda knew Jimmy was trying to get rid of her again, and it made her angry. Was Jimmy lying about work just to put her off? She was tired, fed up with the whole thing. It was time to let him know how he had made her feel. There was one thing in particular that had upset her, and she decided to bring it out in the open.

"Why didn't you tell me Brad was killed and your parents were divorced?"

Jimmy was startled by the question, but most of all by the way Linda asked it.

Linda didn't wait for an answer. "That hurt, Jimmy. I'm sorry about Brad and your parents. Real sorry. But at the same time, I'm really upset with you. You didn't even tell your mother that I was back. We were friends once, good friends, in case you've forgotten. We used to share everything. I think the way you've treated me has been inexcusable. The Jimmy Stillman I remember wasn't rude, self-centered, and insensitive. And that's putting it mildly."

Jimmy was defenseless. Linda was right, and he knew it.

"It's pretty obvious," continued Linda, "that you have your own world now and don't want anyone else in it—especially me. But don't worry, you don't have to avoid me anymore, because I won't bother you. That's a promise." She turned on her heels, then looked back over her shoulder at Jimmy. "And thanks for making me feel so welcome, Stillman. It's been appreciated."

Jimmy felt like he'd been hit in the stomach with a heavy blow. He sank back against the wall and watched Linda walk away. She was right—he had tried to keep her out of his world, but not because he didn't like her. He cared more than he would like her to know; that had always been the case. Seeing her again after so many years was the best thing that had happened to him in a long time. But he knew if he let her into his life again she would discover the ugly secret he had been hiding the past three years. It was impossible to keep anything from Linda—that had been the very reason he quit writing her. To be thought of only as rude and insensitive was easy. He could live with that, but to have her know the truth was unthinkable and unbearable. Now that she was walking out of his life, though, he was confused. Angry and frustrated, he turned, hurried down the stairs, and burst through the doors to the outside. He had to breathe, to think.

# 9

Even if Jimmy had accepted the invitation to go fishing, Linda would have had to cancel. She learned that night that she was expected to attend a Young Women's conference in Ithaca, New York, on Saturday. It was her responsibility to phone the other girls and see who would be going.

When she phoned Allison they talked about the Sadie Hawkins girls' choice dance that was coming up in a few weeks. Allison had heard from one of Beau Taylor's friends that Beau wanted Linda to ask him. *Why shouldn't I?* Linda thought. *There's no one else I want to go with—at least, not anymore.*

Friday morning things went as usual. Jimmy came in late for chemistry, and Campbell marked him tardy as he slid into his seat. Linda shot a look in his direction. She couldn't help it. He was still the best-looking boy in the school, even though he was a jerk.

This morning she thought he looked especially good. His hair was still wet from showering—and it was combed! *Who is he trying to impress?* Linda wondered. He looked so clean and fresh. It was obvious that he had shaved—his face shone, and even his ears were shiny. She turned her attention back to Campbell and his lecture, promising herself she wouldn't look at Jimmy again. He was out of sight and out of mind, as far as she was concerned.

Three rows away, Jimmy's heart was pounding, and the palms of his hands were moist. He was writing a note—to Linda. Once he finished it he folded it as tightly as he could, waiting for the right moment to send it. At ten minutes to nine he looked to the front of the room. Campbell was at the board, his back to the class, writing down the next day's assignment. Jimmy shot a look at Linda. She was copying the instructions that were on the board. Jimmy quickly handed the note to the girl next to him, who passed it on to the next desk.

"Mr. Campbell," someone on the front row called out, "is that page thirty-three or page fifty-three?"

Campbell turned. "Fifty-three." As he was about to turn back to the board, he noticed something out of the corner of his eye.

"Hold it right there!" he demanded.

The entire class came to a standstill.

Jimmy died a thousand deaths. Linda looked up to see what was going on.

Campbell left the board and moved down the row, where he retrieved the note from a smiling student. Waving it in the air, he said, "Ah, more community property! Okay, who's responsible for this one?" No one raised a hand. "C'mon, 'fess up. Who sent the note?"

Without looking up, Jimmy slowly raised his hand. Linda was shocked. Jimmy was sending notes!

"What do you say, class? Shall I read it?"

Once again, it was unanimous. Campbell slowly unfolded the note and read it to himself, then looked up at the class. He raised his eyebrows. "Are you ready for this?"

The class was definitely ready.

"Here we go." Campbell cleared his throat. "Linda . . ."

Linda sat up straight and shot a look at Jimmy. The back of his neck was scarlet, and he was staring straight ahead. She could tell he was in unspeakable misery.

Campbell continued, "I got off work on Saturday if you're still interested. Same time, same place."

The class went wild.

Jimmy was shaking his head.

"Wait," said Campbell, "there's more. It says, 'I'm sorry . . . Jimmy.'"

"The big question here is," said Campbell, joking, "who's bringing the bait?"

The class roared.

After class Linda and Jimmy talked in the hall. Jimmy understood about Linda's conference, and they both agreed that the fishing would have to be put on hold for a while.

"Thanks for the note," said Linda, smiling. "You made my day." She gave Jimmy a quick hug, then hurried off to class. One thing was certain in Linda's mind now—she wasn't going to ask Beau Taylor to the Sadie Hawkins dance.

# 10

The Sadie Hawkins dance was less than two weeks away. Linda had her mind set on asking Jimmy. She was trying to convince Allison to ask David Rowe, the only boy Linda had seen Jimmy talk to since she had returned. *If Dave goes with Allison,* she reasoned, *then Jimmy would feel more comfortable about going to the dance.* He had already accepted her invitation to go fishing, but dancing might be a different story.

So far she wasn't having much luck persuading Allison. It probably had a lot to do with the fact that Allison was five feet ten inches tall and Dave was only five feet four. But the biggest complaint Allison had was about the black leather jacket Dave was never seen without, as well as his form of transportation—the biggest, loudest motorcycle Allison had ever seen or heard.

"There is no way I'm gonna ride to Sadies on the back of a Harley-Davidson with my arms wrapped around a guy half my size," she protested.

"C'mon, Ali, you're missing out on all the fun things in life," Linda argued. "I promise you'll look back on this and remember it as one of the most memorable experiences you had in high school. And don't worry, I'll drive. Besides, what a great opportunity to do missionary work."

Allison rolled her eyes. "With Dave Rowe? C'mon, give me a break."

"Please, Ali," Linda begged, "you do this for me and I'll never ask another favor from you as long as I live."

Allison looked down at Linda, trying to compose a way to say no without hurting her feelings. But her pause was a little too long, and Linda took advantage of it. Just as Allison was about to speak, Linda threw her arms around her and gave her a big hug. "Oh, Allison, thank you; I'll love you forever for this. I owe you a big one."

Before Allison could figure out what had just happened, Linda was long gone.

Now that Linda had the Allison situation behind her, she was faced with one more obstacle—a creative way to ask Jimmy and Dave to the dance. She knew it had to be foolproof with no "escape clause" built into it, because if there was a way out, Jimmy would find it.

Thanks to her good old Uncle Chris, she came up with a colossal idea. Chris just happened to be passing through Towanda on his way back home to Rochester, New York.

Chris was her father's youngest brother and easily her favorite uncle. In fact, it seemed that he was everybody's favorite uncle, even to kids outside of the family. He was the most fun-loving person Linda had ever known. A book could be written on the April Fools' jokes he came up with every year. Linda figured if anyone could come up with a great way to ask Jimmy and Dave to Sadies, it would be Chris.

"Do you know any of the policemen in this town?" Uncle Chris asked Ted.

"My first counselor, Vaughn Potter, just happens to be on the police force."

"Terrific! Okay, here's the plan," said Uncle Chris.

After he shared the idea with Linda he grabbed the phone and asked, "Shall we call Vaughn Potter?" Linda just grinned and nodded.

Vaughn Potter thought the idea sounded like a lot of

fun and agreed to be at the high school the next morning at eight o'clock sharp—in full uniform.

The next call was to Burt Thomas, principal of Towanda High School. Linda was certain that "Stoneface," as the kids called him, wouldn't go along with the plan. Uncle Chris dialed anyway.

"Burt," said Uncle Chris, as if they were long-lost Navy pals, "are you a fun-loving guy?"

Linda buried her face in her hands. This was "Stoneface" he was talking to—the man most feared by every student at the high school. When Uncle Chris laughed out loud, Linda dropped her hands and stared at him in disbelief.

"Little darling," Uncle Chris said to Linda when the call was finished, "you girls better go and curl your pretty hair or do whatever girls do to get beautiful, because it looks like we're definitely on for tomorrow!"

Linda laughed and screamed, throwing her arms around her uncle.

The next morning the parking lot at Towanda High School was teeming with kids, cars, and buses when Vaughn Potter and Uncle Chris pulled up to the school's main entrance in a patrol car. Potter had the siren screaming and the lights on the roof spinning and flashing for added effect. Linda and Allison watched all of this from across the parking lot, crouched down in the front seat of Linda's Toyota. For a split second both of them had thoughts of backing out on the whole thing.

"What happened, Linda, couldn't you get the chief and the entire force here?" Allison asked sarcastically.

"Potts" and Uncle Chris were really hamming it up. They got out of the car at the same time and looked this way and that, with their eyebrows knitted together big time.

"Is your uncle really a police officer?" asked Allison.

"No, he's a paper salesman for Xerox."

"You're kidding." Allison was incredulous.

If Linda hadn't known better she would have been fooled too. The way Potter and Uncle Chris were acting, one would have guessed that half the faculty had been murdered inside and the other half was being held hostage. By this time the parking lot was buzzing with speculation.

When their eyebrows got tired, Potter and Chris decided it was time to make their big move and head into the school. Linda and Allison quickly jumped out of the car and hurried inside, where they beelined it to the restroom to get ready for the command performance of their lives.

When "Stoneface" came over the PA system that morning, a hush fell over the entire student body. The students were certain that the first announcement of the day would let them know why the police were in the school. "James Stillman and David Rowe, please report to my office *immediately!*" The tone of his voice was all business.

At 8:30 sharp Jimmy and Dave entered the main office as planned. They both seemed tentative and nervous, especially Dave. Mrs. Farr, Thomas's secretary, met them at the main counter. "Go right in, boys, they're waiting for you," she told them.

Confused about who "they" might be, Jimmy and Dave slowly moved toward the open door of Thomas's office, where they could see Vaughn Potter seated near the far wall.

When Thomas, Uncle Chris, and Potter saw Jimmy and Dave, they made sure the atmosphere cooled immediately. Sober faces replaced smiles. Thomas was the first to stand and speak.

"Boys, before these gentlemen ask you any questions, I want you both to know you have the right to an attorney." Jimmy shot a worried look at Dave. They both sat down in front of Thomas's desk.

Outside the door Mrs. Farr ushered Linda and Allison into her office, where they could listen to what was going on via the intercom. Thomas was introducing Uncle Chris and Vaughn Potter to Jimmy and Dave.

"Boys, I presume you know Officer Potter of the Towanda Police Department."

Solemnly, Jimmy and Dave both nodded.

Thomas turned to Uncle Chris. "This, boys, is Lieutenant Jack Mitchell from the Scranton Police Department's undercover division."

Uncle Chris glared, scowled, then acknowledged the boys. He was having the time of his life. He reached into his coat pocket and retrieved a small notepad and pencil, then barked, "Which one of you is James Stillman?"

Both boys jumped a little in their seats.

"I'm Jim Stillman, sir," said Jimmy.

Chris looked long and hard into Jimmy's eyes, as though he were trying to read the label on the back of Jimmy's soul. Jimmy shifted uncomfortably in his seat.

"You eighteen yet, son?" Chris spoke with a deep Southern accent that could fool anyone.

"No, sir, not until next month."

"What kind of car do you drive?"

"A 1972 Ford pickup."

"What color?"

"Green, sir."

Chris shot a quick look right at Potter, and both men nodded to one another as if to say, "We got our man." Uncle Chris jotted down a quick note on his pad.

"Where were you on the night of October fourth?"

At that moment Jimmy couldn't remember his name, let alone where he was on the night of October fourth.

"I asked you a question, son!" barked Uncle Chris. "Where were you on the night of October the fourth?"

"I . . . can't remember, sir."

In the room next door, Linda and Allison were on the edge of hysteria.

Uncle Chris shot another meaningful look at Potter. Potter just nodded his head in agreement.

After Chris had jotted down another note, he turned his attention to Dave. "What's your full name, son?"

"David Taylor Rowe, sir."

"And how old are you, David Taylor Rowe?"

"Eighteen, sir."

Uncle Chris's left eyebrow nearly stood on end. A sinister smile washed across his face. He looked at Thomas, then at Potter, then scratched the number eighteen on the pad. He stared at the number, then circled it several times. He looked up quickly at Dave, startling him.

"And what kind of car do you drive, David Taylor Rowe?"

"I don't have a car, sir. I have a motorcycle.

"You know, son," said Uncle Chris, "I'm gonna get real upset if either one of you boys calls me 'sir' one more time. Do you understand?"

"Yes, sir!"

Linda and Allison were in stitches.

"What kind of motorcycle is it that you have?"

"A Harley Davidson, sir."

Uncle Chris glanced again at Potter, who returned the look and nodded affirmatively. Another entry went down on Uncle Chris's notepad.

"And where were you on the night of October the fourth?"

All color drained from Dave's face. He swallowed hard.

"Do I need to rephrase or repeat the question, son?"

"No, sir." Dave looked like he was about to hyperventilate. After a long pause he continued, "If I tell you the truth, will you go easy on me?"

Jimmy jerked his head toward Dave. Linda and Allison stopped laughing and stared at the intercom speaker.

Uncle Chris didn't quite know how to handle this question. He looked at Potter, who was wearing the same bewildered look.

"In my book, son," said Uncle Chris, "honesty is always the best policy. Speak your piece."

"It was me," said Dave, perspiring and sliding forward in his seat. "Jimmy had nothing to do with it. It was a solo job."

All eyes in the room were on Dave.

"I didn't have any money for gas, so I went out to the gravel pit and siphoned some out of one of the trucks. I only got a half a tank when I saw Officer Potter's car comin'. I took the back road through Monroeton and then went home. You gotta believe me, man, I was gonna pay them back out of my next paycheck."

Potter was dumbfounded. He had to turn his head so that Dave couldn't see him smile.

In the next room Allison looked incredulously at Linda. "You want me to go to Sadies with a felon?"

Linda couldn't contain herself any longer and started to laugh.

Back in Thomas's office, Uncle Chris was trying to get things back on track. He turned to Potter. "Officer Potter, do you have any questions you want to ask these boys?"

"No, I've heard enough."

Uncle Chris put the pencil and pad back into his coat pocket and gave the boys a final look, then turned and looked at Mr. Thomas.

"Mr. Thomas, I personally have no more questions at this time. But I do have two other people waiting outside who I would like to bring in."

"Okay." Thomas got up from his desk.

Jimmy and Dave looked at each other, more confused then ever.

On their cue, Linda and Allison rushed into the principal's office. When Thomas opened the door, Linda and Allison stepped in with their heads hung low, looking victimized.

"Young ladies," said Chris, "are these the boys?"

Linda and Allison looked into the eyes of Jimmy and Dave. The boys shot another look at each other, then looked back at the girls.

"Yes," answered Linda.

"That's them," said Allison.

"That's good enough for me," said Uncle Chris. "Do you have any questions you'd like to ask them?"

Linda stepped forward first and looked right into Jimmy's wondering eyes. "Jimmy, would you go to Sadies with me?"

Jimmy's mind was too jumbled for him to answer.

Allison quickly followed suit. "Dave, would you go to Sadies with me?"

"What? Hey, wait a minute," said Dave, "you mean this doesn't have anything to do with the gasoline at the gravel pit?"

"It didn't, but it does now," said Potter.

Mr. Thomas burst out laughing.

"Fellas," said Chris, still with the authority of Lieutenant Mitchell, "answer the question—will you or will you not escort these ladies to the dance?"

"Yeah," said Jimmy, nodding.

Dave just nodded his head, still thinking about the unnecessary confession. Jimmy looked up at Linda. He'd been had and he knew it. The smile that Linda had waited so long for broke out on his face. The twinkle that she remembered was still there.

The week before Sadies, Linda and Allison spent hours shopping to buy matching shirts for themselves and Jimmy and Dave to wear to the dance. The day of the dance they spent all morning and afternoon shopping and preparing food for a special candlelight dinner.

Just after dark on the evening of the dance, Linda picked up Jimmy, then drove back to Towanda for Allison. The three of them drove across the bridge to east Towanda to get Dave. Allison walked to the door, knocked, and waited. Finally Dave's ten-year-old sister answered.

"Hi," she said.

"Hi," said Allison. "Would you tell Dave that Allison is here?"

"Dave's not here. He went out with some of his friends."

"I know you're kidding. Just please tell him I'm here."

As Dave's sister was about to repeat herself, his mother appeared in the doorway. "May I help you?" she asked.

"Hi, I'm Allison Turner and I'm here to pick up Dave for our date to the Sadie Hawkins dance."

Dave's mother stared at her. "I will kill that boy when I get my hands on him," she finally said, slowly shaking her head. "I had no idea he had a date tonight. He left here about an hour ago with friends. I'd go find him and drag him back by the hair of his head if I knew where he was. I'm terribly sorry about this."

"That's okay." Allison turned and started for Linda's car.

Dave's little sister felt sorry for Allison and wanted to cheer her up. She stepped out onto the porch and called to her, "I like your shirt. Dave has one just like it."

Allison didn't answer. She slid into the backseat of the car and closed the door.

"I have never been so humiliated in all my life," she said. "Just wait till I get my hands on that little greaser."

Linda and Jimmy just looked at each other. There was no way they could drop Allison off and go to the dance. So Jimmy made up a story about his foot and how it was too sore to dance because a truck tire had fallen on it that morning at the garage. "If you girls don't mind," Jimmy said, "I'd just as soon all three of us go to a movie."

After a lot of pleading and a few more little white lies, Jimmy and Linda finally coaxed Allison into spending the evening with them. For the rest of the evening it was a threesome, with Jimmy walking with an exaggerated limp. They ate dinner by candlelight at Linda's, then went to the Keystone Theater for a double feature.

As they took their seats in the theater and waited for the lights to dim, Dave Rowe and two friends walked down the aisle past them with . . . dates! To make matters worse, Dave was wearing the shirt Allison had given him.

Allison jumped to her feet. Linda tried to grab her but it was too late—she was already storming down the aisle. Linda covered her face as Allison stepped into the empty row in front of Dave and glared down at him. When Dave looked up and saw Allison he nearly choked on his popcorn. From his point of view, the five-foot ten-inch tall Allison looked seven feet tall at least.

"Take . . . it . . . off!" said Allison slowly and deliberately.

"What?" Dave tried to act casual.

"You heard me." Allison's voice rose. "Take it off!"

The theater was beginning to grow quieter by the moment. People were craning their necks to see what the ruckus was all about in aisle fifteen.

"Look," said Dave, "I'm sorry. I'll make it up to you if you'll just go away and leave me alone."

*"Take it off!"*

"I don't have anything on underneath it," said Dave pleadingly.

"TAKE IT OFF!" screamed Allison at the top of her lungs.

"Okay! Okay!" Dave stood and handed Allison his drink so he could unbutton the shirt. He took it off and handed it over to her.

"There, satisfied? Now, give me my drink."

"Certainly," said Allison, as ladylike as she could. Then, before Dave knew what was happening, she tipped the huge container over Dave's head. Rivulets of red Hawaiian Punch ran down his face and neck and over his bare back and chest. Allison handed the empty cup to Dave, turned, and left the aisle. The movie audience had no idea what was going on, but they loved it. A mighty cheer and enthusiastic applause exploded in the theater as Allison carried Dave's shirt back up the aisle to her seat. Right behind her was Dave's date, hurrying out of the theater.

As the lights dimmed, Allison looked over at Linda. "You were right," she said. "This will be the most memorable experience of my senior year." A smile started at the corners of her mouth and spread across her face. "I've never had so much fun in my life." She threw a chocolate-covered peanut into her mouth and turned to watch the previews.

# 11

The following Monday Linda got the shock of her life. Jimmy had dropped out of school to work full-time! She had heard it through the grapevine, then went straight to the school office, where she had it confirmed. Right after school she raced to Monroeton to the service station where Jimmy worked.

Jimmy was putting gas into a car when Linda pulled up on the other side of the pumps. When he saw Linda he rolled his eyes and shook his head. He had a good idea why she was there.

He finished with his customer and slowly made his way to Linda's car. "Hi, what can I get for ya?"

"I'd like seventy-five cents' worth of gas" Linda said, counting out some coins. "No, wait—make that seventy-eight cents, please. And when you're through with that, would you please check the air in my tires?"

"Sure. How much pressure would you like?"

Linda had no clue how much air went into a tire. "I don't know, just put in the usual."

" 'Bout a hundred pounds in each tire?" said Jimmy facetiously.

"If you think that's enough."

"That should be plenty." Jimmy tried hard not to smile. "Anything else?"

"Yes, please check the battery, the oil, and the transmission fluid and the windshield wiper stuff."

Jimmy went right to work. He moved quickly to the side of the car, where he put in the seventy-eight cents' worth of gas.

"If you'll just pop the hood, I'll check the fluids," he told Linda.

As Jimmy reached under the hood to check the transmission fluid, Linda playfully beeped the horn. It frightened Jimmy, who jerked his head up, bumping it on the underside of the hood. He stepped to the side of the car, rubbing his head, and shot a dirty look at Linda. She shrugged her shoulders and mouthed the word "Sorry."

Linda got out of the car and stood beside Jimmy as he checked the battery.

"Why did you drop out of school?"

"Now, how did I know that question was coming?"

"What could you possibly be thinking about? You're too smart to spend the rest of your life working in a gas station. You've got to graduate. What about college?"

"College isn't for me." Jimmy straightened up. "Battery water's a little low. What kind would you like?" Jimmy teased.

"I don't know, what do you recommend?"

"Cadillac battery water. Just took some out of that Cadillac over there. Looks like good stuff."

"I'll trust whatever you say. Go ahead and put it in."

Jimmy grabbed a pitcher of water from off the top of the pump and filled the battery until it overflowed. He snapped on the caps. Next he pulled out the dipstick to check the oil.

"Jimmy, you have too much potential to do this. You're smart. You were always the smartest kid all through elementary school. You'll be sorry if you don't graduate."

"You don't need any oil, but it's looking a little dirty.

It's probably about time for a change. And the windshield stuff looks okay." He reached up and closed the hood.

"Please don't ignore me, Jimmy," said Linda. "I know what I'm saying is right."

Jimmy turned and faced her. "This wasn't a decision I made over the weekend. I've thought about this for a long time. Things are a little different at my house than they are at yours. My mother's working two jobs just to pay the rent."

"What does she think about your quitting? She can't be going along with this."

Jimmy quickly changed the subject. "I almost forgot to check your tires. Let's see, how much pressure did you say you wanted? A hundred and fifty pounds?"

"I don't know. Whatever."

Jimmy went to work checking the air pressure.

"As soon as I leave here I'm going to talk to your mother," Linda announced.

Jimmy stopped what he was doing and looked up at Linda. His eyes were getting darker. "Leave my mother out of this. She's got enough problems of her own. I mean it, Linda."

"Don't even try and threaten me, Jimmy Stillman. I've never been afraid of you, and I'm not going to start now. And don't tell me that you're doing this for your mother. If the truth were known, your mother would have you graduate and go on to college."

Jimmy got to his feet and glared down at her. She leaned in to let him know she wasn't about to back down.

"What is it with you?" Jimmy demanded. "What do you care whether I drop out of high school or graduate?"

"Because we're friends, and I care about you. Something happened to me in California that opened my eyes. I realize how important life is. It's not something to waste. It's precious. We have to make the most of every day. If you decide to quit high school, your life will never be what it could be."

Jimmy's jaw tightened. "Yeah, well, you listen to me. While you were in California working on your suntan I learned a few things about life too."

Another car pulled to the pumps.

"I'm sorry that my dropping out of high school doesn't work for you, because it's working just fine for me," Jimmy said, holding out his hand. "Seventy-eight cents, please."

Linda took a dollar out of her shirt pocket and slapped it hard into Jimmy's hand. "Keep the change!" She got into her car and drove away.

For the rest of that day and into the night, all Linda could think about was Jimmy. He was so stubborn and bullheaded that she had decided to just forget him and let him mess up his life. She didn't know what else to do. At dinner she discussed the problem with her parents.

"When all else fails, take it to the Lord," her father told her. That was the only thing left to do.

After her prayers that night Linda lay in bed still thinking about Jimmy. *Why won't he listen to me?* she wondered. *He used to listen to me when we were kids. He must see that dropping out of school leads nowhere. He must, because he's smart,* she reasoned. *But why would he want to ruin his life?*

*Why couldn't things be like they were when we were kids? Why do things have to get so complicated when you get older?* she wondered. She and Jimmy had always talked so freely about everything and anything in the old days.

Suddenly she had a flash of inspiration. Why hadn't she thought of this before? She quickly turned on the light and set the alarm clock for 5:00 A.M.

# 12

Early the next morning, before sunup, Jimmy Stillman awoke from a sound sleep to the noise of pebbles pinging and bouncing off his bedroom window. He climbed out of bed, stumbled to the window, and looked out. Below, in the driveway, he could see Linda standing, holding a fishing rod in one hand and a picnic basket in the other. She was all smiles, as though yesterday had never happened.

He opened the window and leaned out into the cool morning air. "What's going on?"

"I'm goin' fishin'. Wanna come?"

"What time is it?"

"Five-thirty."

"It's too early."

"Someone once told me you don't catch the big ones in bed."

"That's the stupidest thing I've ever heard." Jimmy was almost smiling. He rubbed his eyes, then looked back down at Linda. "You're serious—you really wanna go fishin'?"

Linda held out the fishing rod. "Do I look like I'm kidding?"

"I'll make a deal," said Jimmy. "If you don't hassle me about high school, I'll go."

"Deal," said Linda.

"Yeah, right," said Jimmy facetiously as he disappeared back into his bedroom to get dressed.

A few minutes later Jimmy opened the back door and let Linda in. They sat at the kitchen table talking and eating cold cereal like they used to when they were younger. The only thing different was the house. Jimmy and his family had moved from their home on Poplar Street in Towanda to this home in Monroeton when Jimmy was twelve. Linda had loved the house on Poplar—it always seemed so bright and cheery. She glanced around the kitchen as they talked. This house was dark and gloomy, and she could tell by the way it was furnished that Jimmy and his mother were barely making ends meet. When Jimmy's father left, Mrs. Stillman was forced to sell ownership of Stillman's Bakery and had to work all kinds of crazy hours. *What happened to this family?* Linda wondered. *Why did Jimmy's parents get divorced? They always seemed so happy.*

"What are we using for bait?" Jimmy asked between bites.

Linda almost choked on her cornflakes.

Jimmy's spoon stopped midway to his mouth.

"Don't tell me you forgot the bait."

Linda slowly and painfully nodded her head. "Sorry."

Jimmy shook his head and smiled. "That's okay. We'll get some clippers."

"Not those ugly things."

"They're still the best bait there is for catching bass." Jimmy pushed away from the table, grabbed his bowl and Linda's, and put them into the sink. "C'mon, let's go," he said, heading for the door. Linda was right behind him. At the door he took two hats off a rack and put one of them on Linda's head. "Can't go fishin' without a hat," he said, pulling down on the hat's beak until it covered her eyes.

Outside Jimmy grabbed his homemade clipper scoop from the back porch and tossed it into the bed of his pickup before jumping into the cab. Linda climbed in next to him. After three or four tries the old truck started up, and they were off.

They parked behind the old telephone company building, gathered up all their gear and food, crossed River Street and the railroad tracks, and headed down the path to the river. Jimmy threw the scoop and his gear into the boat and got in.

When he turned to help Linda he found her just standing on the shore, staring at the boat. She was pretending this was the first time she had seen it since she returned.

"What's the matter?" asked Jimmy.

"I love this boat. I can't believe you still have it. What does that say on the side?"

Jimmy pretended he didn't hear. "C'mon, let's go," he said. "We still have to get some bait."

"Jimmy," said Linda with mischief in her eyes, "does that say—*The Linda?*"

"Yeah," said Jimmy under his breath as he arranged the gear in the boat.

"You named it after me!" She was really rubbing it in.

Jimmy tried to brush off any sentiment. "I needed a name, and you liked the boat so much I figured, why not? C'mon, let's go. We're wasting time." He reached out and grabbed Linda's hand and yanked her into the boat. Within minutes they were out of Hunsinger's Cove and headed for the small rapids just north of the Towanda bridge.

After Jimmy had anchored the boat in the rapids, he and Linda took off their shoes, rolled up their pant legs, and waded out to where the water ran quick and white and where the hellgrammites, insect larvae that the locals called clippers, hid beneath the rocks.

"Remember how we used to do this?" shouted Jimmy over the rushing water.

"I think so," said Linda.

"Okay, what do you wanna do—lift rocks or catch them in the scoop?"

"I'll catch them in the scoop."

Jimmy handed Linda the wire clipper scoop, which she placed under the water right in front of a large, flat stone. Jimmy positioned himself behind the stone and lifted it, and the swift-moving water carried two plump, unsuspecting clippers right into the scoop.

For nearly an hour they worked the rapids, catching clippers. As the sun was coming over Table Rock Mountain, they had their limit of thirty.

"Any special place you wanna fish?" asked Jimmy.

"You're the expert. Where are we going to have the best luck?"

"The last time I was in Freedom Cove I got two great-looking bass."

"Sounds good. Let's go."

They got back into the boat and Jimmy started to row toward the island. Linda couldn't help but notice how big and powerful his arms had become since the last time she had been in the *Linda* with him. She could still remember how he used to struggle and splash to get across the river or row against the current. Now he and the old boat seemed like one fine-tuned machine.

Before Linda knew it they were on the other side of the island, gliding silently and effortlessly toward Freedom Cove. They anchored in the middle of the cove and fished all that morning. Linda discovered quickly that her years in California had taken the edge off her fishing skills. As usual, Jimmy caught most of the fish, even with the time it took him to bait Linda's hooks and take the fish off her line. They talked a lot about the "good ol' days" and the fun they used to have together. They laughed and reminisced about the time Jimmy wrestled "the monster" and set him free right here in Freedom Cove.

"Of all my memories, that day stands out as the one I will always remember the most," said Linda. "I still can't believe you caught that fish and carried it all the way over here. What did you weigh then?"

"Probably about seventy-five pounds," Jimmy said with a chuckle.

"I can still see you now, standing on the bank, looking down at that huge fish and yelling, 'No fish, no matter how big, is gonna beat Jimmy Stillman, king of the river.' And then you did it. You won. I was so proud and so in—" Linda caught herself just in time before she said "love." Jimmy looked up at her, and their eyes met and held for a moment. She knew she was beginning to blush, and hoped Jimmy didn't notice. "I was so impressed," she quickly said. "Seems like yesterday, doesn't it?"

"Yeah, those were fun times."

"Hungry?" Linda asked.

"I could eat."

"Lunch is served." Linda reached for the picnic basket. They set their fishing poles aside and basked in the warm afternoon sun, eating ham sandwiches and whatever else Linda was able to dig out of the fridge at five o'clock that morning.

After they finished eating Linda leaned back against the rear of the boat and gazed up through the trees, past Table Rock Mountain to the blue sky overhead. The warm rays of the sun and the steady sound of water lapping against the sides of the boat were so relaxing that she slowly dozed off.

Jimmy baited his line with another clipper and cast as far out into the cove as he could, then propped the pole against the side of the boat. He turned and looked at

Linda. He was glad she had fallen asleep, because now he could look at her for more than just a moment. He couldn't believe what six years in California had done to his little fishing buddy. She had turned into a beautiful girl.

He was enjoying the moment so much that at first he didn't notice the pull on his line and the bend of his pole. The pole jerked forward and was nearly yanked right out of the boat, but he lunged for it and grabbed it just in time. On the other end of his line was the biggest smallmouth bass of his illustrious career. After several minutes of battling with the bass, Jimmy reeled it in, then scooped it up by one of its gills and tossed it into the boat. The wood bottom of the boat must have frightened the fish, because it seemed to get new life. It flipped and flopped out of control until it landed right on top of Linda's stomach, where it paused for a rest. Linda woke with a start, letting out a bloodcurdling scream, but Jimmy was laughing too hard to come to her rescue. The bass flipped off of Linda's lap and landed exhausted beside her on the bottom of the boat.

Linda started to laugh too. "It's huge!" she finally said. "That's gotta be a record."

They sat and stared at the exhausted fish for a long time. The bass was at least thirty inches long and easily weighed six or seven pounds. It was a beauty.

"Have you ever seen a smallmouth bass this big?" asked Linda.

"Just once." Jimmy picked up the tired fish and held it in his hands.

"Where?" asked Linda.

Jimmy hesitated for quite some time before he quietly spoke. "I was with my dad just below the James Street bridge when he caught one. I think maybe his was a little bigger." His expression clouded a little. "I wish he could see this one."

"Where is your dad?"

Jimmy didn't take his eyes off the bass. "Last I heard he was living in Scranton."

"Did he remarry?"

Jimmy shrugged. "I don't know."

"What do you mean, you don't know? When's the last time you saw him?"

"He left about three months after Brad's funeral."

Linda was dumbfounded. "And you haven't seen him since?"

Jimmy just shook his head slowly.

"Why?"

Jimmy pretended he didn't hear. He looked at Linda and gestured to the fish.

"I guess we have to let this ol' man go, don't we."

"Why?"

"Because this is Freedom Cove, remember?" He forced a smile but didn't wait for an answer. He released the big fish into the water and watched it swim slowly away. After it disappeared Jimmy turned back to Linda. "That's a good one to quit on, don't you think?" He grabbed the anchor rope and started pulling it in.

Linda sat forward. "Jimmy, can we please talk for just a minute?"

Jimmy continued pulling on the rope. "If it's about my dad, I don't want to talk about him."

"You two were always so close. I don't understand how your dad could just leave and not even keep in touch. Why, Jimmy?"

"I don't know," Jimmy pulled the anchor into the boat.

"Is that the truth? You really don't know?"

Jimmy didn't answer. He laid the anchor on the floor of the boat.

"If you don't want to talk about it, I can accept that," said Linda. "But if you do, you know that whatever you tell me goes no further than right here."

Jimmy stared at the bottom of the boat for a long time. *Sooner or later she'll find out,* he told himself. It was inevitable. He took a deep breath and looked up at Linda, the color draining from his face.

"It was my fault that Brad was killed!"

"What do you mean?" Linda tried to hide her shock. She waited for what seemed like forever before Jimmy spoke again.

"I didn't listen to my dad," he said softly.

Linda sat back and listened while Jimmy told her the saddest story she had ever heard.

"When I was twelve," Jimmy began, "we moved from our house on Poplar Street to Monroeton. We had about five acres. We were raising a cow, some pigs, and a few crops. Things were great then. Dad ran the bakery, and Mom stayed home with us.

"When I was fourteen my dad bought an old pickup to help with the chores on the farm. He let me drive it on the dirt roads and around the property as long as he was with me. He made me promise that I would never drive the truck unless he was sitting beside me.

"One Saturday afternoon Mom and Dad took the family car to Towanda to do their weekly grocery shopping. I can still hear Dad say, 'Think before you act,' as he and Mom drove away from the house. Just as soon as they were out of sight, Brad said, 'Let's take the truck for a ride. Dad'll never know.' I said, 'No, I promised Dad I wouldn't drive unless he was with me.' But Brad never let up, and that old pickup with the keys dangling from the ignition was just too much temptation.

"At first we just drove around the property on the dirt roads. Then Brad said, 'C'mon, let's go down the highway.' I forgot all about my promise to Dad—I was having such a good time I forgot about everything. We were having the time of our lives, with the windows rolled down and the old radio cranked up as loud as it would go. I turned onto the highway. 'Faster, go faster,' Brad kept saying. Something inside was pushing me—it was like I was possessed. We were going about sixty and climbing when Brad said, 'Let me drive.'

"The stupid little kid grabbed at the wheel, laughing. I screamed at him to stop, then pushed him away. The wheel slipped out of my hands. When I looked up we were heading toward the other side of the road. I pulled the wheel hard to the right, but it was too much—we went heading for the barrow pit. I pushed the brake pedal to the floor. Dad had never had the truck inspected because we never took it on the pavement, and the brakes were shot. All's I could hear was the sound of metal rubbing against metal.

"Brad quit laughing. We shot across the barrow pit, and the front end of the truck dropped and we hit right in the middle of the pit. The truck flipped over on its top, and I heard glass breaking all around me. Then everything went quiet.

"I can still hear the quiet. I was on the ceiling of the cab, but I was okay. I couldn't believe it. I can remember thinking, *Dad's gonna kill me.* I called for Brad to see if he was okay. He didn't answer. I looked around, and he wasn't in the cab. I crawled out through the broken window and started calling for him." Jimmy paused and looked at Linda. Tears filled her eyes and spilled onto her cheeks.

"Then, I saw him," Jimmy continued. "He was under the truck. As soon as I saw him I knew he was dead. I felt so helpless. I never prayed before or since, but I got down on my knees and I prayed. 'Dear God,' I said, 'make this a dream. I don't want this. Please help Brad to be alive.' I opened my eyes, and the truck was still upside down and little Brad was still underneath, dead.

"I didn't know what to do. I ran all the way to the Monroeton bridge. I wanted to jump and kill myself, but I was too chicken. I ran up into the woods and hid for about five hours until I got too hungry and cold. Just before dark, I headed down to the highway. I had no place to go but home.

"When I got pretty close to the highway I saw my parents coming up the road in the car, looking for me. They saw me. Dad pulled over and jumped out of the car. He looked different—I knew it was my dad, but then again, it wasn't my dad. He had a look in his eyes that I'd never seen before, and it scared me. I turned and started to run, and he chased after me, yelling out my name over and over. I could hear my mother running behind him, crying and screaming at him to leave me alone and not hurt me. I ran faster. He finally caught me. It was like he was crazy. He grabbed me and shook me real hard and kept screaming in my face. 'Why didn't you listen? Why didn't you listen?' I screamed back at him, 'Go ahead and kill me. I don't care. I deserve it!'

"Then my mother came. She was crying and screaming at my dad, telling him to leave me alone. She pushed him away. 'Don't you know how he must feel?' she kept saying. 'He's suffering enough, can't you see that!'"

Jimmy took a deep breath. "It was so ugly, and it was all my fault. My father looked at me and then at my mother and just turned and walked away. I don't know where he went. He didn't come home that night. The funeral was two days later. After that, things were never the same—they just got worse and worse. None of us talked to each other. I knew that every time Dad looked at me he was thinking about Brad and hating me. I did a lot of fishing back then. He and Mom never got along after that. Then one day about three months later I came home from school and Mom told me he was gone. In some ways I was glad. We haven't seen him since."

Jimmy breathed out a huge sigh. He looked up at Linda, embarrassed and self-conscious, wondering what she must be thinking. Linda sat on the edge of her seat in stunned silence, wiping away the tears. She reached out and touched Jimmy's hand.

"Sorry you asked?" asked Jimmy, forcing a smile.

"No, I'm glad you told me." Everything seemed so clear now—why Jimmy had suddenly quit writing letters to her when she was in California, and most of all, why his personality had changed so drastically. *How did he survive all of this?* Linda wondered. She wished she could have been there to help him through it.

"It's getting late," Jimmy said suddenly as he grabbed the oar handles and began rowing out of the cove.

The boat ride across the river was a quiet one. Linda was pensive—her mind was trying to find solutions to Jimmy's problems. Unless he could learn to forgive himself and put the past behind him, his life would never go anywhere. She had to find an answer—*the* answer.

What Linda didn't know was that her silence was killing Jimmy. His imagination was running wild—he was sure she was thinking terrible thoughts about him. She must be in a hurry to get home, to get out of his life as fast as she could, Jimmy thought. He hated himself. He hated life. He was almost convincing himself that he hated Linda too. He rowed the boat with all his strength, faster and faster. He was glad that it was getting dark so Linda couldn't see the bitter tears in his eyes.

Once they reached the other side of the river, Jimmy quickly secured the boat, gathered his gear, and headed up the bank. Linda had a hard time keeping up.

The ride to Chestnut Street was like the boat ride

across the river—quiet and fast. When they reached Linda's house, Jimmy screeched to a halt. "See ya," he said abruptly as he stared out through the windshield.

"The last time a guy said 'See ya' like that, I never saw him again," Linda joked.

Jimmy didn't respond.

"Look at me, Jimmy."

Jimmy reluctantly turned and faced her.

"Do you know what the definition of a friend is?" She didn't wait for an answer. "It's someone who knows everything about you and still likes you. I'm your friend, Jimmy Stillman." She leaned over and gave the surprised Jimmy a kiss on the cheek. He didn't quite know what to say.

"Now that that's settled," she said. "Come on in for supper. Mom's expecting you."

"I can't, I've got things to do."

She reached over and snatched the keys from the ignition. "Things can wait."

She opened the door and jumped out, then hurried to the front of the truck where she was bathed in the light of Jimmy's headlights. She smiled and gestured for him to hurry. Jimmy looked at Linda for a moment, then turned out the lights and slowly followed her into the house.

# 13

The hills surrounding Towanda that October were a kaleidoscope of oranges, yellows, and reds. Linda loved the change of seasons in the East, but autumn had always been her favorite time of year. She wanted to share it with her friends in California, so she gathered the most brilliantly colored leaves she could find, boxed them up, and mailed them off. She was falling in love all over again with Towanda, but most of all, with Jimmy Stillman.

Ever since Jimmy had shared his tragic story with her, he and Linda had become the closest of friends again. It was just like old times. During her lunch hour Linda would drive to Monroeton to be with him. Any time Jimmy had off at the service station was spent with Linda. On weekends they were inseparable. The more time she spent with him, the more she liked him. And the more she liked him, the more she wanted him to know about the gospel. But what if he wasn't interested? The awful thought had kept her from asking him. She knew she had to put her fears behind her and just ask him the next time they were alone together.

On the last Friday night in October, Jimmy invited Linda to go deer hunting with him the next morning. No matter what, she decided, Saturday would be the day she would pop the golden question.

The next morning they left at dawn and spent most of the day in the hills outside of the small town of Dushore. It was buck season, and Jimmy had promised Linda's father that if he tagged one he would share it with the family. Dressed in bright orange jackets and hats, Jimmy and Linda hiked through the hills looking for a prize buck. They saw a lot of does and a few fawns that afternoon, but no bucks.

Then suddenly their luck changed. A little after four o'clock Jimmy had decided to call it a day and head down the mountain to his truck. As they reached a clearing on the mountainside Jimmy spotted the biggest buck he'd ever seen. It was about one hundred yards away, moving straight toward them. Without taking his eyes off the buck Jimmy grabbed Linda by the shoulder and yanked her to the ground behind a fallen tree.

"What's the matter?" Linda asked, alarmed.

Jimmy put a finger to his lips; then, with a jerk of his head, motioned toward the buck. Linda craned her neck and peered up over the log. The sight of the beautiful creature took her breath away. Gracefully, cautiously, silently, the huge deer glided in their direction.

As quickly and quietly as he could, Jimmy rested the barrel of the rifle on the fallen tree, then scooted himself forward where he could get a good bead on the deer.

Linda watched with wild anticipation as Jimmy froze in position with his right eye staring down the barrel of the gun and his right index finger wrapped carefully around the trigger. She could hear her heart beating. Her eyes shot to the deer, which was less than forty yards away now, and she watched in silent awe as the huge animal high-stepped through the tall grass. It was so beautiful and magnificent.

Suddenly the buck stopped. Perhaps it had heard something. Perhaps it had caught their scent. It turned, ears twitching, eyes darting. It was in the perfect line of fire.

"Beautiful. . . . Now, don't move, big fella," Jimmy whispered. He was trembling with excitement. He took a deep breath, held it, then aimed for the buck's heart and slowly squeezed the trigger.

At the last possible moment Linda reached over and bumped the stock of the gun just as Jimmy pulled the trigger. The noise from the discharge reverberated throughout the small valley and echoed off the far mountain. The big buck bolted away unharmed and disappeared into a nearby thicket.

Jimmy got to his knees and watched, crestfallen, as the trophy buck vanished into the woods. He turned and glared at Linda. "What'd you do that for?" he demanded.

A sheepish look came over Linda's face. She shrunk back against the log, trying to think of a good reason. "Didn't you see the movie *Bambi?*" She smiled weakly.

"What!" Jimmy was incredulous.

"Sorry," said Linda. "He was just so beautiful and defenseless standing there. I didn't want to see him die."

Jimmy sat back on his haunches and leaned against the tree. He took off his hat and ran his fingers through his hair, staring down the mountain.

Linda's mind was racing, trying to think of something to say to warm Jimmy up. She slid a little closer.

"Try and think of it this way," she said. "I saved you a lot of time and trouble. Now you don't have to carry that big thing down the mountain."

Jimmy just closed his eyes for a moment and slowly shook his head.

"What if he had a wife," Linda continued, "and little fawns waiting for him to come home—and then he never came home? How would they feel?"

Jimmy turned and looked at Linda. He half smiled and shook his head.

"I'm sorry," said Linda. "Forgive me?" She clasped her gloved hands under her chin and raised her eyebrows, trying to look as innocent as she could.

"If you had it to do over again," asked Jimmy, "would you have done the same thing?"

Linda thought for a moment. "To be honest, yes."

"That's not true repentance. I heard that in one of the talks at your church." Jimmy turned away again and stared up at the sky.

"Tell you what," said Linda. "I'll try and make it up to you. I'll treat you to something to eat on the way home." She smiled and snuggled closer to him.

Jimmy smiled back but didn't answer. He looked into her eyes and started to forget about the trophy buck that got away. Her eyes, he thought, seemed to dance when she smiled. Today they looked even more blue than he had ever remembered. He studied her face. The cool mountain air had painted her cheeks a soft pink. She was the most beautiful girl he had ever seen; that he was certain of.

Linda noticed Jimmy's eyes move to her mouth, then back to her eyes again. She was getting flustered, and Jimmy knew it. The smile on her face slowly melted away as Jimmy moved closer, and she felt as though he was looking right through her, reading her thoughts. She wanted to look away but couldn't. Everything seemed so still, so quiet—except for her wildly pounding heart. She hoped Jimmy couldn't hear it.

Jimmy reached out and put his hand around her waist. As he leaned in to kiss her Linda stammered, "Shouldn't . . . we go?"

Jimmy stopped, his face almost touching hers. "Why?"

Her mind drew a blank. Jimmy didn't wait for an answer. He leaned in to kiss her for the first time.

"That was the biggest deer I've ever seen!"

The voice rang out from somewhere behind them, breaking the spell.

Jimmy and Linda got to their feet quickly as two men in their forties, carrying guns, stepped out of the woods. "How you missed that one I'll never know," said the first man.

As they drew closer the other hunter spoke up. "Next opportunity you get like that, son, make the most of it." He winked at Jimmy as he and his friend passed by and headed up the mountain trail.

Linda flashed Jimmy a sheepish grin and shrugged her shoulders. Jimmy smiled and grabbed the beak of her cap and pulled it down over her eyes. "C'mon, let's get outta here," he said. "I'm hungry, and you owe me dinner." He put his arm around her and together they walked down the mountain.

About a half hour later Jimmy and Linda emerged from the woods onto a dirt road where Jimmy had parked the truck. He opened the door for Linda but then paused.

"Hold still," he said.

"What's the matter?"

"Nothing. You've got something caught in your hair." He stepped closer and began picking out a few loose leaves.

Linda liked being this close to Jimmy. She looked up at him and studied his face. She loved his jaw—it was so square and strong.

"Look at you," said Jimmy playfully. "I invite you to go hunting, and you go and get yourself all dirty."

"It's all your fault for pulling me down like that."

Jimmy picked one last blade of grass from her hair. "There, got it."

"Thanks," said Linda.

"No problem." Their eyes met. Jimmy was looking at her the same way he had earlier on the mountain.

Linda's pulse quickened. "I think I just heard those hunters again," she said nervously.

Jimmy's eyes never left Linda's. "They're on the other side of the mountain by now."

He moved closer and kissed her softly.

When he pulled away, Linda was in a daze, eyes still closed. She opened them and looked at Jimmy, who was looking at her with an amused smile. Her mind raced for something to say.

"Would you like to hear the missionary lessons at my house on Sunday night?" she finally blurted out. Instantly she was horrified. *What a stupid thing to say after being kissed!* she thought to herself. *He must think I'm a real airhead.*

"What time?" said Jimmy, still amused.

His voice brought her back to the moment.

"What did you say?" asked Linda, confused.

"What time Sunday night?"

"Seven o'clock!"

"Sure, why not." Jimmy grinned as he pulled her close and kissed her again.

# 14

When Jimmy arrived at Linda's house on Sunday evening he was given a warm welcome by Linda, her parents, and the missionaries. He liked the elders immediately. Elder Fairfax, a recent convert from Riverside, California, was a handsome, powerfully built young man who had passed up a full-ride football scholarship to serve the Lord for two years. When he stood to meet Jimmy he flashed him a contagious smile that reminded Jimmy of a piano keyboard.

"Hey, what's happenin', dude?" he said, shaking Jimmy's hand enthusiastically and slapping him on the shoulder. Jimmy felt right at home.

Elder Rigby, a potato farmer's son from Snake River, Idaho, was a hard worker who had saved all his earnings to support himself on his mission. He taught Jimmy about Joseph Smith and the Book of Mormon. When he had finished he bore a strong testimony of the book and challenged Jimmy to read at least one chapter of it a day. "Pray and ask God if it's true," Elder Rigby counseled him, "and at the same time, ask to know if Joseph Smith was really a prophet."

Jimmy said he would.

Elder Fairfax slid forward in his chair. "James, my man," he said, "football was my life. I ate it, I slept it—it's all I ever thought about. I never went anywhere without my football. I used to go to class with it; I took it on dates. I even showered with it. Everybody thought I was crazy. But I wasn't crazy; I was focused. I had a goal—to be the best I could be. The last thing on my agenda was to be away from the pigskin for two years preachin', but—"

Suddenly Fairfax became very serious and soft-spoken. The room went deathly quiet.

"I read the Book of Mormon and asked my Heavenly Father if it was true and if Joseph Smith was his prophet. He answered me in the affirmative. As sure as I'm sitting here, Jim—it's true. Believe me." He picked up his scripture case. "When I decided to go on a mission, some of the returned missionaries on the team at Ricks College took that football I told you about, and look what they did to it." He held out his scriptures for everyone to see. The case was made from the same leather that was once his football. "James, now I know what's really important. Everywhere I go I take these with me"—he waved the scriptures in his hand—"because I'm focused. I want to be the best I can be. And I want you to be the best you can be. You pray about it, and you'll know."

Jimmy committed himself to reading the Book of Mormon and praying about it, and even said he would come back for another lesson the following Sunday. Linda went to bed that night with high hopes.

The next Sunday Rigby and Fairfax got the shock of their missions.

"Well, Jimmy, how did it go this week?" asked Elder Rigby. "Did you read and pray about the Book of Mormon?"

"Yes, I did," said Jimmy.

"How many chapters were you able to read?" asked Fairfax.

"I read the whole book."

Rigby and Fairfax shot surprised looks at each other. They couldn't believe it.

Fairfax couldn't contain his happiness. "James . . . my man!" he exclaimed, laughing.

Jimmy told them he had prayed about it and had received the answer that it was true. Linda threw her arms around him and gave him a big hug.

That night the discussion was centered around the love of Christ and his atonement and resurrection.

"Because Christ loved us so much, Jim," Rigby explained, "he died for us. If we live worthily and keep his commandments, we can have all that is his."

As the lesson progressed, Linda noticed a change come over Jimmy—a change she didn't like. He became quiet and inward, not at all like himself.

After Elder Rigby gave the closing prayer Jimmy was the first one to his feet.

*His good-bye sounds so final,* Linda thought. She walked him outside to his truck.

"Is something wrong?" she asked.

"No, I've just got a lot on my mind, that's all. I'll call you tomorrow." He got into his truck and drove away.

Jimmy didn't call the next day, or the next. On Wednesday during lunch Linda drove to Monroeton to see him. He was in the station's garage, getting ready to change the oil in a pickup truck. He looked so unhappy.

He looked up and spotted Linda, and it startled them both. Linda waved, and Jimmy waved back, but didn't smile.

Linda stepped into the garage. "I thought you were going to call me on Monday."

"Sorry," said Jimmy. "I've been swamped."

Linda watched as he reached up under the truck, which was raised on a hoist, and drained the dirty oil into a pan. "What have you been swamped with?"

"Work."

"Don't you get off at five?"

"Yeah," said Jimmy.

"Sunday night after your lesson, when you said you'd call me the next day, I knew you wouldn't. Don't ask me how I knew, but I did. And I'm wondering—if I hadn't called or come down here today, would you have ever called me again?"

Jimmy didn't answer. The oil had drained from the truck. Jimmy screwed the plug back in; then tightened it with the wrench.

"Would you have, Jimmy?"

"Of course I was going to call you."

"When?"

Jimmy walked from under the truck to the hoist controls. Linda followed him, waiting.

He released a lever and the truck slowly descended from the ceiling to the cement floor. "I was going to call and say good-bye." His voice was quiet.

"Good-bye?" Linda was shocked. "Where are you going?"

"Into the army."

"The army? But why?"

"Because there's nothing here for me."

"Oh, thanks a lot." Linda pretended she was kidding, but she was hurt.

"You've been a great friend, Linda. But in six months or so you'll be out of here and off to BYU. What do you want me to do, hang around here and wait for you to come home from college so we can go fishin'? I've got my own life. I've got to make plans for myself."

"When's all this going to happen?"

"I have a meeting with the recruiter on Monday."

"What about your mother? What does she think about all this?"

"She's not too crazy about the idea, but she'll get used to it."

The truck was firmly on the ground now. Jimmy raised the hood and propped it up. He removed the oil cap, then turned and grabbed a push-in oil-can spout and four quarts of oil from a shelf directly behind him.

"What about the lessons with Elder Fairfax and Elder Rigby? They're going so well."

"I think those guys are great, but if I kept taking the lessons I'd just be wasting everybody's time."

"I thought you said you knew the Book Of Mormon was true."

"I thought it was interesting. And I'm glad I read it."

"No," said Linda adamantly, "you said you read it all and prayed about it and knew that it was true. Didn't you mean it?"

Jimmy didn't answer. But Linda could tell he was getting frustrated with her by the way he pushed the metal spout into the can of oil. He poured the first can into the engine.

Linda watched him, her hands on her hips. "You're running away, aren't you?"

Jimmy didn't respond. He removed the empty oil can and threw it into the garbage. He rammed the spout into the next can and began pouring it.

"Don't you have to get back to school?" Jimmy said sarcastically.

"Nope," said Linda, getting back at him for being so mean. "I can cut all my classes if I want to. I'm getting As in all of them."

The thought of Linda hanging around the station all afternoon quizzing him didn't exactly thrill Jimmy, and Linda knew it. Jimmy's jaw tightened, and he threw the next empty can into the garbage with even more force. It rimmed out and rolled across the floor, leaving a thin trail of oil.

"Missed," said Linda.

Jimmy forced the spout into the next can and shoved it hard into the engine. As he waited for it to empty, his fingers played an impatient drumroll on the radiator.

Linda didn't say a word as Jimmy emptied the final can into the engine and slammed the hood down. He faced her and spoke. "What do you want from me?"

"Just the truth."

"I've told you the truth."

"That's a lie, and you know it."

Outside the bell sounded as a car pulled up to one of the gas pumps.

"Saved by the bell," said Linda sarcastically.

Jimmy glared at Linda before spinning around and walking outside. Linda went into the office and watched through the window as he gassed up the car. He knew she was watching but made sure he didn't look her way. When the car drove off, he turned and walked slowly back into the station. He closed the door and sat down on a chair across from Linda.

"I can't join your church," he said.

"Why?"

"I just don't feel good about it. I've caused too many people too much grief to think I can be baptized and have everything forgotten, just like that."

"What happened to Brad was a mistake," said Linda.

"Tell that to my father," Jimmy said angrily.

"Weren't you listening at all Sunday night? Christ paid for all of our sins and mistakes. If you've sincerely repented, you can walk away and have everything forgotten. Everything!" Linda drew closer to him, and her voice became gentle. "He's our big brother, Jimmy. He wants to carry our burdens for us if we'll just let him. You are valuable—Christ died for you! He loves you. It's time to unload and go on with your life. You can put it behind you and start over."

Jimmy looked up from the floor at Linda. If only it could be as easy as she was making it sound.

"Christ isn't the only big brother we have, you know," Linda continued. "We have another one named Lucifer. He wants you to do just what you're doing—to run away from the truth and never forgive yourself for your brother's death. Lucifer had his chance and blew it. He wants us to do the same thing."

She stopped talking and looked at Jimmy. She felt good inside about what she had said—it was right and true. Jimmy looked away. He too had felt something and couldn't deny it.

"As for me, Jimmy Stillman, you're not going to get rid of me that easily. Whatever you decide to do, I'll always love you and be your friend. No matter what."

Without saying good-bye, she turned and walked out the door.

Jimmy watched until she drove away. Frustrated, he kicked the garbage can across the room, then slumped back into his chair and stared aimlessly into the garage.

# 15

"Directory, this is Patty. What city, please?" said the operator.

"Scranton," said Linda.

"How may I help you?"

"Do you have a number for a Jack Stillman?"

"One moment, please."

*This is a long shot,* Linda thought to herself. She was certain Mr. Stillman no longer lived in Scranton.

The operator returned. "I have a Jack Stillman on 438 Watson Avenue."

"That's him!" Linda exclaimed. She quickly jotted down the address and the number.

For a long time afterward she sat motionless in the chair, staring at the phone and wondering what Jimmy would do if he knew what she was up to. It didn't take much wondering. *He would wring my skinny neck, that's what he'd do,* she decided. But she didn't care. This was the right thing to do. She jumped up and hurried into the kitchen, where she left a note on the counter for her mother:

Mom,
Be back around seven.

—Love,
Linda

It was around three o'clock in the afternoon when Linda pulled out of the driveway and headed in the direction of the Towanda bridge. The drive to Scranton would take just over an hour. She turned on her favorite radio station and began rehearsing to herself what she would say to Mr. Stillman.

Watson Street was a narrow little road on the west side of Scranton that meandered along the Delaware River. Four hundred thirty-eight Watson was in an old green apartment complex that sat precariously on the side of a steep hill. A rickety set of wooden stairs, overgrown with weeds, climbed the hill to a porch.

Linda parked the car by the side of the road, then leaned forward and looked up at the porch, where she could see an old man sitting in a rocking chair. *He looks harmless,* she thought. She got out of the car and locked it. As she made her way up the old stairs she said a silent prayer that she would be able to say the right things and that Mr. Stillman would listen and understand.

When Linda reached the porch she looked at the old man and said hello. He flashed her a toothless grin and nodded his head.

"Is this where Jack Stillman lives?" Linda asked.

"Yes it is, sweetheart. He's in number four—second door at the top of the stairs. Just got home 'bout ten minutes ago."

"Thank you," said Linda as she stepped through the front door.

As she climbed the stairs, huge butterflies with monstrous, flapping wings filled her stomach. At the door she paused, took a deep breath, and threw back her shoulders. She knocked three times and waited.

Through the closed door she could hear footsteps coming to answer her knock. Her heart was pounding. The door opened, and there stood Mr. Stillman, looking much older than Linda had remembered. *He looks sad,* Linda thought as she looked into his eyes.

"Yes, can I help you?" he said.

"Mr. Stillman, I hope you remember me. I'm Linda Mooney. Your son Jimmy and I were close friends before I moved to California."

Mr. Stillman took a step back. "Linda, I can't believe it's you!" he exclaimed, smiling. Linda felt relieved. Her confidence was back.

"Please, come in," he said as he opened the door wider and gestured for her to enter.

Linda stepped into the front room of the small apartment. Mr. Stillman closed the door behind her, then hurried to a ragged sofa and began clearing it of newspapers and several pieces of clothing.

"Here . . . please, have a seat. I'm sorry the place is such a mess, but my housekeeper just got home ten minutes ago." He laughed nervously as Linda sat down on the sofa. Mr. Stillman crossed to a wooden chair and sat down across from her.

"What brings you to Scranton, Linda?" he asked.

"Jimmy," said Linda.

Mr. Stillman's expression clouded as he leaned forward in his seat. "If you're looking for Jimmy, I believe he and his mother still live in Towanda." He hesitated a moment. "I haven't talked to Jimmy or his mother for about three years." He sank back into his chair.

"I've seen Jimmy," said Linda. "My family and I moved back to Towanda in September. And I do know that you haven't spoken to him for a long time. That's why I'm here."

Mr. Stillman braced himself.

"Jimmy has never forgiven himself for Brad's death, Mr. Stillman. He blames himself for the divorce. He believes that you hate him and that he has ruined his mother's life. That's a pretty tough burden for a seventeen-year-old boy to carry around. The fact that you haven't spoken to him in so long has just about destroyed him." Linda's eyes were filling with tears, but she didn't care.

"Jimmy is the finest boy I have ever known or even met." Her voice cracked with emotion. "He's intelligent, he's handsome, and he has a wonderful heart. He could be anything in life that he wants to be. But because of the way he feels about himself, he's trapped in a box that he can't escape. He's dropped out of school and headed nowhere."

Linda looked long and hard at Mr. Stillman. She could feel her anger rising.

"He was only fourteen years old, Mr. Stillman. What happened was a mistake. It was a mistake! If Jimmy could relive it over again he would never have gotten into that stupid truck. He loved Brad!" She was crying now. "None of us can even imagine what Jimmy must think about when he's all by himself. He must be one of the strongest people alive. I don't know how he has gone on. I know I couldn't. You're probably upset with me for coming here today, but I'm the only friend Jimmy has. And I thought maybe if you knew what Jimmy was going through, you might be able to help. You must care, Mr. Stillman. Jimmy is such a good boy." She waited for a response, but there was none—at least, not for the moment.

What happened next was something Linda hadn't expected and wasn't prepared for. She thought she noticed tears welling up in Mr. Stillman's eyes, but before she could tell, Mr. Stillman lowered his head and shielded his face with his right hand. She could see his Adam's apple moving up and down. He was crying, and trying hard not to let it show.

Linda was confused. This couldn't be the unfeeling, unloving father that she had imagined. Mr. Stillman turned his head away and brushed away the tears. After he had composed himself he turned back and looked at Linda. He cleared his throat and finally spoke.

"It wasn't Jimmy's fault that Brad died; . . . it was mine."

Linda leaned back in the sofa and listened as Mr. Stillman painfully told her his side of the story.

It was true, she learned, that Mr. Stillman had told Jimmy not to drive the truck unless Mr. Stillman was with him. "As we set off for Towanda to do our grocery shopping that afternoon, Mrs. Stillman told me that I'd better take the keys out of that old truck because 'the boys were just that—boys,' and the temptation would be too great. I didn't listen. I ignored her repeated warnings and drove off to Towanda. If I'd listened to her that day Brad would still be alive, and our lives would have gone on as before.

"When I saw Brad under that truck I couldn't look at my wife. I knew what she was thinking, I knew what she was feeling about me. We searched and searched for Jimmy and finally found him coming out of the woods. The guilt I felt was crushing me. I had to blame someone. Jimmy was the one. I chased him down, grabbed him, and kept screaming at the top of my lungs, 'Why didn't you listen? Why didn't you listen?' I was really screaming at myself. I let him go and just walked away and kept on walking. I must have walked twenty miles that night, then turned around and walked back into Towanda and stayed the night at a motel.

"During and after the funeral I could never find the right words to say to my wife or to Jimmy. I had ruined everything. Our relationship slipped and slipped until it was like we were all strangers. None of us ever talked. Jimmy stayed clear of me. He was never home when I was, and I was never home when he was. You're right, he probably thought I didn't love him anymore.

"I didn't know what to do except vanish from their

lives. One afternoon I left a note for my wife and left. I came here to Scranton because this is where I was raised, and I got a job at a bakery doing the only thing I know how to do."

Mr. Stillman looked right into Linda's eyes. The sadness in his own dark eyes reminded her of the same sadness in Jimmy's. "I want you to know," he said, "that you couldn't be more wrong, Linda. I love Jimmy. Leaving that day was the hardest thing I've ever done, but I honestly believed it was the best thing for everyone."

There was a long pause as Linda and Mr. Stillman looked at each other.

"You have to tell him how you feel," Linda finally said. "If you could tell him exactly what you've told me here today, it would mean everything to him."

Mr. Stillman didn't respond. He ran his fingers through his hair and just stared at the floor. He was thinking, and Linda thought he looked scared.

# 16

Sunday morning Linda phoned Jimmy. He told her he was still planning on meeting with the army recruiter the next morning. She also learned that he had given notice at the station. If all went as planned, Jimmy could be leaving in less than a week for basic training in Kentucky. Linda invited him to dinner later that afternoon—it was to be his farewell dinner.

Toward evening, after a late dinner at Linda's house, Linda suggested to Jimmy that they go for a ride. "Where do you wanna go?" he asked.

"Why don't we go up to the high school parking lot and just talk?" said Linda.

The parking lot at Towanda High School was situated above the town, where the view was spectacular. When Jimmy and Linda arrived the lot was empty except for a late model sedan, parked about ten yards from where Jimmy parked. In the sedan was Mr. Stillman. He was alone, staring out at the vista. Linda had planned everything—the dinner, the drive—and now this.

"Beautiful, isn't it?" said Linda, looking over the trees to the river. She wasn't really looking at the view; she was looking at Mr. Stillman and waiting for him to do something. "When I was in California I almost forgot how beautiful all of this was."

"I guess when you live here all the time you kinda get used to it," said Jimmy. Just then Mr. Stillman opened his door and got out of his car, appearing nervous and apprehensive. He looked right at Jimmy's truck, then closed the door. Jimmy looked up. Linda swallowed hard and held her breath, wishing she could make herself disappear. Jimmy looked briefly at his father, then back at Linda. And then, suddenly, something registered in Jimmy's mind—
*That's my father!*

Jimmy jerked his head and looked back at Mr. Stillman, his face draining of all color. He looked at Linda again, and his eyes were darker than she had ever seen them. Beads of perspiration appeared on his forehead, and he breathed faster and faster. "You did this, didn't you?"

"Yes!" Linda blurted out. She leaned her back against the door, trembling.

"Why? I don't want to see him! I never want to see him!" He reached for the keys to start the engine, but Linda grabbed them and held them behind her back.

"Give me the keys, Linda."

"No! Not till you talk to your dad."

"I've got nothing to say to him. He ruined my life."

"I thought you said you ruined his life."

Jimmy held out his hand. "Give me the keys."

"He loves you, Jimmy."

"You don't know what you're talking about."

"I only know what he told me."

"He hates me!" Jimmy shouted.

Linda sat up and shouted right back. "Does it make it easier for you to think that so you can go on feeling sorry for yourself?"

"He walked out on us!"

Linda motioned to Jimmy's father. "Look, he just walked back in, and he wants to talk to you and let you know the truth about how he feels. He had his reasons, Jimmy."

"It's too late!"

Linda touched Jimmy on the arm. "You don't mean that. You love him, Jimmy—so much that just the thought of him hating you has almost destroyed you. He loves you. He told me so yesterday. He walked away because he thought it was the best thing for you and your mother. He made a terrible mistake, and he knows it."

Jimmy was fighting back tears.

"He blames himself for Brad's death," Linda said gently. "He blames himself for everything."

Jimmy turned from her and looked out through the windshield, making sure he didn't look at his father. Hot, angry tears streamed down his face.

"I know one thing," said Linda. "If you don't get out of this car and talk to your dad, nothing will ever change. Nothing—and then it *will* be too late."

She dropped the keys on the seat next to Jimmy. Jimmy clenched his jaw, gripping the steering wheel so tightly his knuckles turned white. He looked at Linda, then at the keys.

Linda held her breath as she heard the keys slip into the ignition, and her heart slowly began to sink. She waited, dreading to hear the sound of the engine starting. But instead she heard the door handle click and the door swing open and close. She sighed a huge sigh and started to cry. Looking up through her tears, she watched Jimmy walk slowly toward his father, who stood straight and tall, trying to hide his nervousness. It seemed he wasn't sure what to do with his hands—one moment they were in his pockets, the next, fumbling with his shirt. He finally held one hand with the other. As Jimmy came closer Mr. Stillman forced a smile that soon melted into a look of sorrow—sorrow and pain. He shook his head regretfully.

Linda could tell from Mr. Stillman's reactions that he was amazed at how much Jimmy had grown. Jimmy was easily four inches taller than his dad. Linda could just barely make out what they were saying through the open window. For a long time it was simply small talk—talk about the weather, Penn State football, fishing, and again, how tall Jimmy had grown. By this time the sun had set in the western sky and the overhead lights in the parking lot had turned on.

When the small talk ran out, Jimmy and his dad just looked at each other. Jimmy began to fidget. Linda sat forward in her seat and whispered, "C'mon, Mr. Stillman, tell him what you told me yesterday . . . please."

Jimmy said good-bye to his dad, then turned and started for his truck. Mr. Stillman's hands dropped hopelessly to his side. He couldn't bear to drive back to Scranton alone, knowing that he missed this golden opportunity to let Jimmy know how much he loved him. He called to Jimmy. Jimmy stopped, then turned and walked slowly back to his father. And then, just as Linda had hoped and prayed, the purpose of this meeting began to unfold.

She sat transfixed as Mr. Stillman quietly and humbly expressed his love. He told Jimmy that he was so deeply sorry he didn't know how to express himself. Then he bowed his head and wept. It was the first time Jimmy had seen his father cry, and he was completely disarmed. He stepped closer and placed a comforting hand on his father's shoulder. Mr. Stillman looked up at Jimmy, then reached out and embraced him. Jimmy instinctively wrapped his arms around his father and held him tightly.

Linda watched through tears as father and son tenderly laid to rest their troubled and sorrowful past. A sweet healing and forgiving reconciliation had taken place.

Jimmy didn't say a word as he drove Linda back to her house. He was reliving and relishing every precious moment he had spent with his father. When he pulled into Linda's driveway he didn't bother to turn off the ignition. There was a long pause before Linda finally spoke. "I guess this is good-bye."

"What do you mean?" asked Jimmy.

"You've got that appointment with the recruiter."

"I won't be able to make it. I'm goin' fishin'."

"Fishing?"

"Yeah," said Jimmy, smiling. "With my dad. He's driving back tomorrow morning and we're goin' fishin'." His smile widened and his eyes twinkled. It was contagious— Linda smiled back.

Jimmy reached over and took Linda's hand and gave it a squeeze. "Thanks, California."

Linda just nodded and smiled, then slid out of the truck.

She stood in the dark and watched Jimmy back out of the driveway. She couldn't remember when she had been so happy. Suddenly Jimmy threw on the brakes and drove back toward Linda. He opened the door and stepped out.

"Hey, I've been thinking," he said. "Think you could arrange it so I could start taking the missionary lessons again?"

Linda wanted to shout for joy at the top of her lungs, but somehow she managed to hold it in.

"Sure," she said calmly. "I'll get right on it."

"Thanks." Jimmy got back into the truck and drove away.

Linda was shivering from the cold and the excitement. She hugged herself, trying to keep warm, and watched Jimmy's truck disappear down the street. When she could no longer see it she turned and walked toward the house.

In her heart she knew that tonight she had witnessed the end of a dark chapter in Jimmy's life and the beginning of a new one full of hope and promise.

# 17

All through January Jimmy took the discussions from Elders Rigby and Fairfax. His testimony of Joseph Smith and the restored gospel was sound, and baptism was inevitable. In February Jimmy surprised everyone when he showed up for his fifth lesson with his mother. Jimmy had been doing some missionary work of his own.

"That's all he talks about," said Jimmy's mother. "He got me reading the Book of Mormon, and I must say I am interested."

"Could you guys give her the first discussion? Like you gave me?" Jimmy asked the elders.

Fairfax flashed that winning smile and said, "James, my man, of course we can."

By the end of the lesson Mrs. Stillman agreed to work toward baptism by reading, praying, and attending church. Jimmy gave the closing prayer and asked that his mother receive the same testimony he had received.

Everyone, especially Jimmy, was dealt a big blow the next Sunday. Elder Fairfax sadly announced that he was being transferred the following week and wouldn't be able to continue teaching Jimmy or his mother. When Jimmy said good-bye at the end of the meeting, he and Fairfax embraced one another as brothers. "James, my man," Fairfax said with tears in his eyes, "When you get to BYU, make sure you look me up and I'll dedicate my first touch-down to you. Have we got a deal?"

Jimmy just nodded and smiled.

Fairfax was replaced with a tall, skinny basketball player from Provo, Utah, named Derek Smith. Towanda was Smith's first area, and Jimmy and his mother were his first contacts. He was still learning his discussions, so Rigby did most of the teaching.

The following Sunday after sacrament meeting the missionaries took Jimmy and his mother to the baptismal font to show them where they would be baptized.

Later that night, after the missionaries had left, Jimmy and Linda bundled up and went for a long walk up York Avenue and finally across James Street bridge. Jimmy was happy and talkative. He talked mostly of the gospel and getting baptized. Linda enjoyed just listening.

"Do I have to be baptized in the font?" Jimmy asked.

"I don't think so," said Linda. "I think you can be baptized anywhere you want, as long as it's deep enough that you can be completely under the water."

Jimmy thought about this for a long time. "Good," he finally said, "because there is another place I'd rather be baptized."

"Where?"

Jimmy looked down at her as though he was afraid to answer.

"Tell me," said Linda. "Where?"

"You're gonna think I'm crazy."

"No I won't. C'mon, tell me."

"In Freedom Cove."

"Freedom Cove! This time of year? You'll freeze," Linda said, laughing.

Jimmy smiled and shook his head. Linda looked up at him. She could tell he was serious.

"So much has happened to me there that it just seems right," Jimmy said.

They walked for a long time without talking—just walking and thinking. The more Linda thought about Freedom Cove, the more she liked the idea. Even the name—Freedom Cove. It was the place—the only place.

It was set. The following Saturday, Jimmy and his mother would be baptized. Mrs. Stillman decided to be baptized in the chapel font, "like normal people do."

The weather on Saturday was clear and cold. The river was calm. At one o'clock in the afternoon, Jimmy, his mother and father, Linda and her parents, Elders Rigby and Smith, and several ward members met at Hunsinger's Cove. Several good-size outboard motorboats were on hand to take everyone across to the island. Jimmy had already made it known beforehand that he would row his little row boat, the *Linda*, to Freedom Cove. He wouldn't have it any other way.

"You sure that thing's safe?" asked Elder Smith half jokingly.

"This boat's never leaked a drop in all the years I've had it," said Jimmy.

Linda noticed that Jimmy and his dad shared a look.

Three boats, including the *Linda*, launched from Hunsinger's Cove and headed for the island. Another boat remained behind to carry latecomers across.

What a beautiful sight it was that day, with Jimmy and Elder Rigby dressed in pure white, crossing the river. Cars slowed on the bridge, their drivers sensing that something special was happening.

Within a half hour the party had made it to Freedom Cove. Linda's dad presided over and conducted the meeting. The group sang "I Know That My Redeemer

Lives," and Linda opened with prayer. Elder Rigby talked about faith and repentance. Next, Linda's father gave a short talk on baptism. Since Jimmy was to be confirmed right after his baptism, Elder Smith talked about the gift and companionship of the Holy Ghost.

Just as Jimmy and Elder Rigby were about to step into the water, a familiar voice rang out from behind them. "James, my man!" Jimmy turned. There was Elder Fairfax, dressed in white, coming down the bank. He was smiling from ear to ear. Jimmy shot a look at Linda. She was laughing and crying at the same time. She and her father had gotten special permission from Elder Fairfax's mission president for Elder Fairfax and his companion to be there. Jimmy and Fairfax embraced so hard that it probably frightened all the fish out of Freedom Cove.

"You look good in white," said Elder Fairfax, beaming.

"So do you," said Jimmy.

But no one was beaming more than Elder Rigby. The arrival of Elder Fairfax meant that he didn't have to get into the freezing water.

"Are you ready for this?" Elder Fairfax asked Jimmy.

"I think I was ready the first night you and Elder Rigby taught me."

"Then let's do it," said Elder Fairfax. He stepped into the water and walked out into the cove until he was in waist deep, then turned and faced everyone. A big smile washed across his face. Everyone broke into smiles.

"Bishop," said Elder Fairfax to Linda's father, "when this is all over I want to have a personal talk with the custodian. This is the coldest water I've ever been in."

Everyone laughed.

Fairfax motioned for Jimmy to enter the water and come to him.

"I've changed my mind. I think I'll get baptized in the font after all," Jimmy kidded.

More laughter as Jimmy eased himself into the cold, muddy water.

As Linda watched Jimmy slowly move through the water to Elder Fairfax, her mind raced back to the day Jimmy had freed that big old carp. She could still see him standing there waist deep in the water. *How our lives have changed!* she thought. She had moved three thousand miles away and found the truth, and now she was back and Jimmy was being baptized. It was all meant to be. She glanced up at the sky. A warm, wonderful feeling came over her. Without a doubt she knew that a loving Father in Heaven was watching from above at that very moment, smiling. He had been watching all the time—all through the years. She knew it just as sure as she was standing there on the bank of Freedom Cove.

The sound of Elder Fairfax's voice brought her back to the present. She looked down at the water where he had his right arm to the square, reciting the baptismal prayer. "James Garrett Stillman, having been commissioned . . . " When he finished the prayer he laid Jimmy back into the water and completely immersed him. When Jimmy came up out of the water, he was glowing. The first person Jimmy looked for was Linda. She was smiling through her tears. As their eyes met and held, her mind recalled and echoed words from an earlier time.

"Why are you smiling?" a younger Jimmy had asked as he and Linda huddled beneath Jimmy's boat, protecting themselves from the pounding rain.

"I don't know," said Linda. "I guess I'm just happy. I think this is the best day I've ever had."

After Jimmy was confirmed by Elder Rigby, Linda's mother closed the meeting with prayer. A beautiful, warm spirit had been present. Everyone congratulated Jimmy, and they walked back to the boats and headed across the river for home.

Jimmy rowed the *Linda* back toward Hunsinger's Cove and Linda sat across from him, watching him. *At last,* Linda thought, *Jimmy is at peace with himself.*

"Cold?" she asked.

"Nope," Jimmy said. "I've never felt better."

And Linda knew he meant it.

# 18

The weeks that followed Jimmy's baptism were happy ones. Jimmy and his mother spent every spare minute reading the scriptures and learning all they could about the gospel. Wonderful changes were taking place in their lives. For the first time in over three years Mr. and Mrs. Stillman were communicating again. Jimmy hoped that because of his example his father would one day agree to take the missionary discussions and be baptized too. But in spite of all the good things that were happening to Jimmy and his family, something still troubled Linda. More than anything she wanted Jimmy to get on with his education, but she didn't quite know how to bring it up. Thanks to others who also cared about him, she didn't have to.

One day in April a letter arrived from Elder Fairfax, addressed to Jimmy in care of Linda and her family. When Linda saw it she snatched it off the kitchen counter and headed for Monroeton.

Jimmy opened the letter right on the spot and read it to Linda.

James, my man!

How's everything in God's country? As you can see from the return address, I'm living in Provo and going to BYU. It's beautiful here. The snow has melted in the valley, but the mountains are still snowcapped. Does Table Rock Mountain still have snow on it? Just kidding, my man—I couldn't resist that one. You really need to get out here and see what real mountains look like. Anyway, I'm enjoying myself immensely out here. I went in to see Coach Edwards (head football coach) and they are going to give me a full ride, like they said. I meant what I said about dedicating my first TD to you.

The main reason for this letter, my man, is that I've been thinking a lot about you lately. From the very first time I saw you I knew you were special. Now that you know who you really are (a child of our Heavenly Father) and what life is all about, you've got to start focusing. It doesn't matter what's happened in the past; the future is where it's at. You're smart; you've got potential. Get your education, and be all that you can be. Don't think for a minute that . . .

Jimmy stopped reading out loud and read on to himself.

"What's the matter?" asked Linda.

"Nothing."

"Why did you quit reading?"

Linda noticed that Jimmy was starting to blush.

"C'mon, keep reading," she said.

Jimmy looked at Linda, took a deep breath, and started again.

Don't think for a minute that Linda is going to settle for a guy who works in a gas station in Monroeton. I know you like her, Jimmy. I mean, who wouldn't. She's sharp, she's smart, she's beautiful, and best of all, she digs Jimmy Stillman. Think about what I'm saying and then write me back and let me know all about your big plans.

Your brother,
Link Fairfax


"I always knew Elder Fairfax was smart," Linda said, smiling.

"You didn't have anything to do with this, did you?" asked Jimmy.

"The last time I talked to Elder Fairfax was the night he left."

Jimmy stuffed the letter back into the envelope. It was obvious that he was doing some serious thinking.

"I'd say the Lord's trying to tell you something," said Linda.

Jimmy just looked thoughtfully at her, then at the letter.

"Gotta go," said Linda, getting to her feet. "I promised my mother I'd only be a few minutes." She moved to the door. "Call me later tonight and let me know all about your big plans." She was out the door before Jimmy could hit her with the rag that was in his back pocket.

Later that night, just as Linda was about to hop into bed, Jimmy called.

"What's going on?" he asked.

"Nothing. What's going on with you?"

"Not much," said Jimmy.

There was a long pause.

"I've been doing some thinking."

"About what?" Linda pretended to be naive.

"I was stupid for dropping out of school."

Linda restrained herself from saying, "I told you so."

"Anyway, if I could I'd try and graduate in June, but it's too late. I could probably take some classes this fall and get my diploma around the first of next year. I'm gonna do it."

"Maybe the teachers at the high school would let you make up the work you've missed," said Linda.

"No way," said Jimmy. "I've missed too much."

"Well, it wouldn't hurt to ask."

That was the way they left it.

The next day Linda took it upon herself to talk to every one of Jimmy's teachers, including the senior counselor, Mrs. Phillips. Right after school she drove to the station, where she found Jimmy filling out a state inspection sticker for a car he had just inspected.

"Hi," said Linda, sitting down across from Jimmy.

"Hi," Jimmy said, looking up.

"I talked to all of your teachers today."

Jimmy stopped what he was doing. "What'd they say?"

"I've got good news and bad news. Which would you like to hear first?"

Jimmy slid forward in his chair. "Tell me the bad news first, then cheer me up with the good news."

"Well," said Linda, "the bad news is, every one of your teachers practically fell on the floor laughing when I told them you wanted to graduate in June."

"They obviously don't believe in repentance," said Jimmy.

"Not deathbed repentance," Linda said kiddingly.

"Okay, cheer me up with the good news."

Linda sat forward in her seat. "I talked to the senior counselor, Mrs. Phillips, and she said you could get your diploma by June if you took the GED Test. It would take a lot of studying, but she thinks you could do it."

"What's the GED test?"

"The General Education Diploma test. If you get a seventy percent or higher on it, they'll give you your diploma.

Passing the test is equivalent to graduating from high school."

"How tough is it? Did she say?"

"Mrs. Phillips said you shouldn't have any trouble if you can find the time to study. While I was there she looked up your ACT scores. You did so well she thinks that with your diploma you could get into BYU."

"When is this test?" Jimmy had a glimmer of hope in his eyes.

Linda pulled a pamphlet out of her pocket, opened it, and scanned the information. "Seven o'clock in the morning on May twenty-ninth."

"Where?"

"Mansfield State Teachers College. The Madison Building, room 221."

Jimmy leaned back in his chair and stared at the ceiling. Linda could tell that he was excited. There was hope.

"That's only a little more than four weeks away." Jimmy looked back at Linda. "Think I could do it?"

"If anyone could, it would be you. Remember what Elder Fairfax used to say—'James, my man, you've gotta focus.'"

Jimmy did focus. Every waking moment was spent with his face buried in a textbook. At a college bookstore in Elmira he and Linda purchased some GED sample test booklets. With Linda timing him, Jimmy took every test in every booklet. In the areas where he was deficient he doubled his study time. He was determined to succeed.

Two weeks before the test he went to work studying with Linda for her final exams. When Jimmy's teachers found out what he was trying to do, they rallied around him and gave Linda extra textbooks for Jimmy to study. Together Jimmy and Linda crammed for every exam. Whether they were in the car, at the station, at Linda's, or on the river, they were quizzing each other constantly. They studied so much that there didn't seem to be a question about any of the subjects that they didn't know.

Jimmy's confidence soared when Linda received her grades for her final exams. She was number one in every class except one, where she received the second highest score. Jimmy was ready. Friday night before the test, he set his alarm and went to bed early so he would be fresh and alert the following day.

# 19

Linda paced the front porch, waiting for Jimmy. He was supposed to pick her up at six o'clock. It was now six-fifteen. *Where could he be?* she wondered. She was beginning to panic. The GED test was going to start at seven o'clock sharp, and it was a good forty-minute drive to Mansfield State Teachers College. If Jimmy missed the test, there would be no chance of his getting into college in the fall. Linda wished he would arrive soon so they wouldn't have to hurry. It had poured like crazy the night before, and the roads would no doubt be slippery.

At 6:25 she frantically phoned Jimmy's house. Jimmy's mother answered on the first ring.

"Mrs. Stillman, this is Linda. Where is Jimmy?"

"He had a terrible time getting his truck started and left about ten minutes ago. He should almost be there."

Linda hung up the phone. *If I run down the hill and meet him at York Avenue it will save time,* she thought to herself. She dashed out of the house and ran as fast as she could. Just as she reached the corner of York and Chestnut she could see Jimmy's truck round the corner by the old Episcopal church. He was flying. She hurried to the center of the road and began waving her arms. Jimmy spotted her, threw on the brakes, and came to a skidding stop on the wet pavement. Linda jumped in and Jimmy pushed the accelerator to the floor. The old truck's tires spun, then grabbed, causing the truck to fishtail.

"I couldn't get the truck started," he said as he straightened out the truck and headed in the direction of north Towanda.

"I know, I called your mother," said Linda, trying to catch her breath. She glanced nervously at her watch. "It's six-thirty and it takes forty minutes to get there."

"Tom Childs and I made it in twenty-two minutes once."

"Just be careful, okay?"

"Okay."

"Have you got all the information, like what building and room and stuff?"

Jimmy's expression suddenly went blank. "Darn, I knew I forgot something."

Linda panicked. "Tell me you're kidding, Jimmy . . . Please."

"I'm kidding."

"How could you do that to me?" Linda screamed. "I'm already a basket case and you're telling me you don't know where the test is."

"Relax, everything's gonna be cool. I said a prayer."

Linda slowly turned her head and looked at Jimmy. He actually meant it!

At five minutes after seven the truck came to a screeching halt in front of the Madison building on the campus of Mansfield State Teachers College.

"Just run in," Linda ordered. "I'll park it."

"Okay, okay." Jimmy jumped out of the truck and sprinted into the building.

Room 214 was packed with kids already taking the test when Jimmy hurried in. He moved as quickly as he could to the front of the room, trying hard not to disturb anyone. The person in charge of administering the test was a Mrs.

Buxton, a short, blocky woman with a tolerance level of around zero. With one eyebrow arching to the ceiling she looked at her watch, then at Jimmy with utter disdain for being eight minutes late.

"Car trouble," Jimmy whispered. "Sorry."

Buxton just shook her head in disgust and pushed a test booklet at him. He took the booklet, found one of the remaining seats, and started to dig in.

Meanwhile, across campus, Linda had found the library. Before going in for some serious magazine study, she closed her eyes and offered a simple, quiet prayer. "Dear Heavenly Father," she prayed, "please help Jimmy during this test. He has worked so hard. . . ."

Jimmy worked frantically, trying to make up for lost time. It seemed that every time he looked at the clock the hand had jumped a half hour. It was now nearing nine o'clock. For the past ten minutes Buxton's eyes had been riveted on her stopwatch. At the precise moment the minute hand touched the number twelve, she shouted, "Stop!" shattering the silence and scaring most of the test takers half to death. When Jimmy closed his booklet, he noticed that in the rush of the moment he had failed to write his name and other required information on the booklet cover. As he worked, the other students took their papers to the front of the room where they laid them in a big pile on Buxton's desk. When Jimmy finished, the room was all but empty. He took his test booklet to the front of the room. As he was about to lay it on top of the others, Buxton stepped in front of him.

"I'm sorry," she said, "but you went over the allotted time. I cannot and will not accept your test. You'll have to take it the next time they offer it."

"But I didn't go overtime. I was just writing down information on the cover."

"It didn't appear that way to me. I'm sorry. If I let you

hand in this test, I will be cheating you out of a very important lesson—a lesson that is in many ways more important than everything you have studied to pass this test. I refuse to carry that kind of a burden on my shoulders. Now, if you don't mind I have an appointment at ten o'clock, which you can be sure I will be on time for."

Jimmy panicked as Buxton began gathering her things. He had done all he could do. When Buxton turned her head away from Jimmy he silently offered a quick prayer for help. Just as he said "amen" the door of the room opened and Linda walked in. She could tell immediately from Jimmy's expression that something was wrong.

"How'd it go?" she asked with a hopeful smile.

"Not so good," Jimmy said. "She won't let me turn my test in because she thinks I kept working on it after she said stop. But I didn't; I was just filling out the information on the cover."

Linda turned to Buxton. "Ma'am, won't you reconsider? If he says he didn't go overtime, you can believe him."

Buxton let out an exasperated sigh and shook her head. "My instructions are not to accept any tests after nine o'clock. I have never allowed a test to be handed in late, and I have no intention of making an exception. Where I come from we were taught to obey rules, and that is exactly what I intend to do. I'm sorry."

Linda looked at Jimmy. She had to do something. But what?

"Wait a minute," said Linda. "Was filling in the information on the front cover included in the time you gave to take the test?"

Buxton was beginning to run out of patience. "No, it wasn't."

"Then," reasoned Linda, "he didn't take any longer than the rest of the kids." For a moment Jimmy's hopes soared.

Buxton folded her arms and glared at Linda. "He kept working after I said 'stop.' He says he was just filling out information. I say he was trying to finish the test."

"Couldn't you just believe him and make an exception, just this one time? Please?"

"No! Now, please excuse me," said Buxton, turning to the stack of tests. It was final, and Linda and Jimmy knew it. As Linda watched Buxton organize the more than two hundred test booklets, her face suddenly brightened. Taking the text booklet from Jimmy, she stepped closer to Buxton.

"There is one question I failed to ask you," she said.

Buxton looked up in surprise. Jimmy was all eyes and ears.

Linda spoke slowly and deliberately. "Do you have any idea who this young man is? Whose test you have so blatantly refused to accept?"

Jimmy stood tall and looked Buxton square in the eyes.

For just a split second Buxton's confidence seemed to wane. She looked a little more closely at Jimmy, wondering if perhaps he was the son of someone of great importance.

"I have no idea who he is or where he's from. I don't make it a point to get to know these students. I just administer the test."

"Good," said Linda. She took Jimmy's test booklet and quickly shoved it in the middle of the stack.

Buxton was incredulous, and so was Jimmy. A huge smile broke out on his face. Buxton was beside herself. "What have you done?" she screamed, lunging for the pile and trying to somehow retrieve Jimmy's booklet. But instead she sent the two hundred-plus booklets sailing off the desktop and sliding and scattering across the floor.

"C'mon," said Linda, grabbing Jimmy by the hand and pulling him toward the door.

"Come back here," screamed Buxton, her face scarlet. "You can't do this! Come back here!"

They ran down the hall and burst outside through the doors of the Madison building, then ran down the stairs and across the lawn to where the truck was parked. They jumped in, out of breath and laughing.

Linda handed the key to Jimmy, and he quickly shoved it into the ignition and turned it.

The truck grinded, sputtered, and died. Jimmy and Linda quit laughing.

"Try it again," said Linda, one eye on Jimmy and the other on the front door of the Madison building.

Jimmy turned the key again and frantically pumped the accelerator. The truck almost caught. "C'mon, c'mon c'mon," Jimmy pleaded. All at once, the engine caught and roared like a lion.

"Yes!" shouted Jimmy. He popped the clutch and the truck lurched forward and down the street.

On the edge of town, near a small park, Jimmy pulled the truck over and shut off the engine. Linda looked over her shoulder through the rear window.

"Don't worry, nobody followed us," said Jimmy. "I made sure of that."

Linda sank back against the seat, exhausted from all the laughing and running.

"You know how I felt running out of that building today?" she asked.

"How?"

"Just like that night we ran off the Third Street bridge after the Larkin brothers dropped that pumpkin. Remember?"

Jimmy nodded, smiling. As Linda sat staring through the windshield, catching her breath, Jimmy turned and regarded her for a long moment, reflecting back over all the years he and Linda had been friends.

Linda turned and caught Jimmy looking at her. "What are you thinking?" she asked.

Without warning, Jimmy scooped up Linda with his right arm and pulled her close and kissed her.

"Wo," she said with a smile, trying to catch her breath. "What did I do to deserve that?"

"Everything. If it wasn't for you I'd be pretty depressed right now. You were incredible back there. You've always been incredible."

"Ditto," said Linda.

"I'm—" Jimmy took a deep breath, and Linda thought she could see a hint of tears in his brown eyes.

"I'm just so happy right now," he said. "I don't know what I would have done or what would have happened to me if you and your family hadn't come back to Towanda. For the first time in a long time"—Jimmy choked on his words—"I'm happy. Really happy." A tear spilled onto his cheek. "Look at me, I'm crying like a baby and I don't even care." He laughed. "It feels good."

The warm, wonderful spirit that was present reached out and touched Linda's heart. She listened as Jimmy continued. "I know I feel like this because of Christ's love for me and being baptized and everything. I feel like I've got some potential now. I feel like I can do anything. College is gonna be a piece of cake, and who knows—maybe I'll be able to serve a mission." He turned and faced Linda. He was smiling through his tears. "I love you, Linda. I think you're awesome."

Linda felt so much love in her heart that she moved closer and threw her arms around Jimmy. "I love you too."

They held each other for a long time, just laughing and crying.

Linda was the first to speak. "Did I hear you right? Did you say you were going to go to college?"

"That's what I said."

"Then you think you passed the test?"

"I killed that test."

"I'm so proud of you!" Linda exclaimed as she squeezed him again. "Let's celebrate."

"What do you want to do?"

"Let's go fishin'!" Linda said with a grin.

"You're on," said Jimmy, laughing, as he turned the key and fired the engine. The old truck pulled back onto the road and headed toward Towanda and the blue-green waters of the Susquehanna.